The Office of Future Storytelling

The Office of Future Storytelling

Neil Powell

Copyright © 2022 Neil Powell

The moral right of the author has been asserted.

Apart from any fair dealing for the purposes of research or private study, or criticism or review, as permitted under the Copyright, Designs and Patents Act 1988, this publication may only be reproduced, stored or transmitted, in any form or by any means, with the prior permission in writing of the publishers, or in the case of reprographic reproduction in accordance with the terms of licences issued by the Copyright Licensing Agency. Enquiries concerning reproduction outside those terms should be sent to the publishers.

This is a work of fiction. Names, characters, businesses, places, events and incidents are either the products of the author's imagination or used in a fictitious manner. Any resemblance to actual persons, living or dead, or actual events is purely coincidental.

Matador
Unit E2 Airfield Business Park,
Harrison Road, Market Harborough,
Leicestershire. LE16 7UL
Tel: 0116 2792299
Email: books@troubador.co.uk
Web: www.troubador.co.uk/matador
Twitter: @matadorbooks

ISBN 978 1803132 617

British Library Cataloguing in Publication Data.
A catalogue record for this book is available from the British Library.

Printed and bound in Great Britain by 4edge Limited
Typeset in 11pt Garamond by Troubador Publishing Ltd, Leicester, UK

Matador is an imprint of Troubador Publishing Ltd

Part One

1

We sat back to admire, in the darkened theatre, on a video screen above the stage the giant image of a typewriter. The machine itself, mounted below on an empty desk, illuminated by a column of light. Simultaneously two hands appear, as though bursting from the sleeves of a black jacket. Clack-clack! The armatures of the machine hammer against the trapped paper. A glow makes the man discernible; in late middle age, in self-absorbed activity. Grace enters, carrying a glass of water. She carries it *gracefully* up to the desk where the Storyteller sits. He turns, taking the page out of the typewriter. With another sheet, he hands it to her. She studies both and then reads.

"'Dear Mr Storyteller. I like all your stories, but the one I like most is *Crumb*. Rosie seems like such a nice girl and is faced with such an awful situation. Have you ever thought about reviving this character? I would love it if she was the subject of your next book'." Grace then exchanged the letter for the Storyteller's reply.

"'Dear Anna. Thank you for your letter. It's been a long

time since I thought about this story. To be honest with you, once I finish a book, I don't often return to the characters. But in this case, I promise you I will give it some thought. If I do return to Rosie Crumb, I will be sure to let you know. Thank you again for your letter'."

"I got a letter, asking me if I'd revive the characters," said the Storyteller.

"Bold," said Grace. "You should ask her to adopt a puppy." Studying the Storyteller, she asked, "Are you considering it?"

"Well, I'm thinking about it, yes."

"It will be your last book," she said.

"Yes."

"Is that what you'd want to write?" By that time next year, he would be retired, and no more books. It was his last chance to say what he wanted. "You should really think about it." Grace left him.

The Storyteller signed his reply and then dutifully pulled the collection off the shelf and flicked through the pages. *Crumb. What had happened to Rosie Crumb?* he wondered.

———•———

"Rosie sat in the hospital bed. Her dark hair and small round face held at the centre of the soft pillow. Her father could barely look at her without trembling. A hand in his pocket, the other clasped to the back of his neck. 'Rosie…' he said, the hand sliding to face. (We, the knowing reader, whisper, 'Ice and fog.') The declaration alive in her eyes that matched the colour of her dark hair said, resisting him, 'Dad. You're not getting in.' And now look, she smiled." *The Storyteller's fingers and thumbs separated the pages.* "If it wasn't a boy they'd found for her.

"'This is Leo,' the nurse said.

"'Hello, Leo,' said Mr Crumb. He shook the boy's hand. 'This is my daughter, Rosie.' They all looked at Rosie.

"'I've brought a book to read,' said Leo. The reason for Leo being there? A blinding pain in his head that lit up the world. Leo Harker went to the hospital with a pain in his head. He didn't know why. It was just there when he woke up, a pain in his head. He went to school where he tried to ignore it. He even played in the school football match. But then several badly controlled passes landed him in trouble with his peers. 'Come on, Leo!' they said, calling out their frustration. The next ball went straight past him. The boy fell to his knees, covering his face, awkward glances were made to the coach, the whistle was blown.

"'Leo, look at me. Take your hands away. Tell me what's going on?' In his mind the vivid blur of a football match, the thud of the ball, the stud-raked turf, remained until a blinding flash. The coach pulled away Leo's hands revealing a pair of eyes beset by mirror fragments of the people gathered around him. There was an eye and an eyebrow floating kaleidoscopically around a head, football boots and muddy knees, and a parade of identically folded arms.

"'We're going to A&E.' Coach lead him from the pitch and sat him in the passenger seat, setting off, leaving the rest on the field. (The final score was three nil to their opponents from Hawks Cross.)

"'I'll call your parents,' he said, breathlessly, as he navigated the streets. At the hospital Leo met doctors.

"'You say that words were playing hide and seek, swimming over the page. Sounds to me like you're having a migraine, Leo. We'll do some tests, but I think you'll be fine. Just fine. We'll give you a painkiller, and set you up, okay.'

"While he was waiting for the results, which were *bound*

to be just fine, the nurses, the next morning that is, seeing an opportunity in Leo, took him to see Rosie. A young girl with a broken leg, come in at about the same time. Her mother had been driving. That was enough, really. United by time at the junction beside Layton Gap. But anyway, we shouldn't. The nurses asked him to bring with him the book he'd been reading, that he tried to protest wasn't his. He'd borrowed it from the boy in the next bed.

"'What are you here for?' asked Rosie.

"'Prosopagnosia caused by migraine,' said Leo. 'It means face blindness.'

"'Is it permanent?' she said. 'Can you see me?' Her own eyes focusing on him clearly.

"'Yes,' said Leo. 'I just had a pain in my head. But it's gone now.' Leo Harker spent the afternoon reading to her. The thing which brought Rosie to life was not the sound of his voice, but something quite incidental: a fly behind the bed trapped against the windowpane. They both watched it buzz and dance. After a moment, Leo took a plastic bottle and covered it.

"'I'm not going to kill it,' he said, and slid behind it a piece of paper, carrying it to an open window. The act of setting it free, that was what seemed to wake her. When her father, Mr Crumb, came back, and it was time to leave, Leo asked, 'Do you want anything, Mr Crumb?'

"'No,' her father replied. 'Thank you, Leo. No.' Describing him, while he was still present, 'A nice boy.'

"'Are you in love with her?' the boy who'd given him the book said, when he returned.

"'No,' said Leo. 'She's only fourteen.'

"'Guys fall in love with girls that young in Shakespeare,' the other boy said. 'You were with her all day.' Leo learned that the boy had come in with his grandparents to have a swollen appendix sorted. He lived with them because his mother lived in Paris. He said he wanted to be an English teacher, which seemed so ordinary. It made Leo think of his father and specifically his father's shed in the garden with the roof that opened up to the sky, and the lens inside that his Dad said put his eye to, and the blob of Saturn. How everything was small when you looked at other planets. And did the boy know that five billion years from now the sun would explode?

"'And all the Art there was would be gone,' the boy replied."

———•———

The Storyteller looked up (and we upon him), set the book aside and ponderously pulled the cap off a pen.

"That cocky know-all boy, well, now he was going to be called Eric." He scribbled the name and drew a circle around it; the character brought by name into being. Then ran a hand through his hair.

"An English teacher at Davenport College." The Storyteller saw that this earlier work had possibilities not evident when he'd written it. He wound a blank sheet into the typewriter. Then he stretched his fingers. *You still needed fingers.* 'That cocky know-all boy,' he typed. And then, for inspiration, 'Shakespeare...' The clackety-clack machine gave him a page, which he stopped to read carefully, pressing his fingers to his lips. The zealous typewriter had adopted the habit, as if to prove it was still game, of whenever he used a punctuation mark of putting a hole through the paper. He rose, thinking again about Anna's letter, thinking about the page, thinking about the story, to press it against the window, illuminating the dot pattern with moonlight. The whole idea of ending his career with a reader's request seemed to the Storyteller both apt and ridiculous.

"What are you doing?" his wife said, seeing him by the window.

"Look," he said. "Have you seen the moon? Look how bright it is." *He remembered a piece from Othello:* 'It is the very error of the moon; she comes more near the earth than she has wont — '

"Yes," said Grace. They regarded it. "You can see why insects confuse it with the sun," she said. And then, "What do you want for dinner?" He thought of the fly going up to the moon.

"Oh, I'm not fussy," he smiled.

"I'll remind you of that." She reached over to touch the punctures in the sheet. Now, all there was for him to do was work it out.

2

A good job getting rising star Roy Jenkins to play Eric. In the role the tall handsome actor looked suitably pale and dishevelled, as you'd imagine a teacher to be after a day in the classroom. This was to be our first meeting with adult Eric, sitting in his office. Reading the email, FYI we'd like someone to do it. A competition. The college wanted someone to enter. He reset his glasses, picked up a pen and wrote down on a scrap of paper, 'Storyteller.' And then circled it. Eric held his face for a moment. He was about to make an important decision. He looked up at the office clock. But that was enough. He swept some essays into his bag and switched off the light.

At home on the hallway table he settled his keys, then turned on the TV before filling the kettle. At the sliding door at the back of the living room, he lit up a cigarette and put it to his lips. There he stood contemplating it again. All the teachers at Davenport College got it, *Write a Play*. The itch to participate had surprised him. It would be about this city, if he did. He tapped away ash. That seemed right. He closed his lips again around the filter. Moving his eyes to scrutinise the watch on his wrist. His daughter would be home soon, Eleanor. She was coming back from the Larks' house, which was only five minutes down the road. By the miracle of chance, they'd been born on the same day. Father and daughter. A date that would arrive in a few weeks. It would be her nineteenth birthday and his forty-second. They'd been kids, when she was born.

"Hi, Dad!" she called. Her voice found him at the door.

"Hi," he called back. He heard the front door close and her feet climb the stairs. He taught English at Davenport College. The kettle in the kitchen rumbled to a boil, and he dropped the cigarette.

3

Two weeks later. Eric sat in his study, focused now, redrafting the first act. Eleanor's face appeared at the door. He looked up.

"You all right?" he said.

"Yes." She then regaled him with what had happened at the Larks' house. Richard's younger brother, Alex, had caught her in the bath, which had created an almighty 'fucking fuss' in her words. With Rebecca Lark in hysterics. Like her mother, Madeline, Eleanor did not suffer fools. We'll talk about Madeline later.

"Are you hungry?" Eric asked.

"Yeah." Eleanor then lay downstairs on the sofa. She concluded that the world was weird and the people in it were weird too.

"Your girlfriend says you should be there for seven," said Eleanor on hearing Eric's feet in the hallway.

"Okay," he laughed. A birthday party was being planned

for them by the Larks. There was something about Rebecca Lark, you see.

"Why don't we go out for lunch tomorrow?"

"Okay." She dipped her spoon into the bowl beneath her chin. Anyway, it was all right now. She switched on the TV for the news. It was predictable fare, until they got to the story about the couple in Sweden responsible for defacing the art gallery. This was important.

"Dad!" she called him. It was reported that the pair had watched endlessly *Love It Be Love*, a hugely popular film. The news showed footage of Maja and Elias being led away, but not before the chance came, before they were out of sight, for Maja to give them a starlet's smile.

"Why did they do it?" Eleanor asked, her tongue lingering on the metal, turning to her dad.

"I don't know," said Eric. The reason for their actions seemed to be an innocent word, twice repeated in a four-word title. His face bore a frown and his glasses then got pushed up over the bridge of his nose. Eleanor watched him. This was a situation where he played the part of a professor so well. She had asked (which was also the reason why she studied her father so intently that evening) because the woman they were due to interview was his mother. A woman held in a unique category. A virtual stranger for much of Eleanor's life (and Eric's too, as it happened), but there she was, more real than real – an image, live on their TV screen.

"Have you spoken to her, Dad?"

"No," he said, smoothly. But who wouldn't be curious about this woman? 'Who's your grandmother?' 'Who's your mother?' 'She's this painter.' 'Wow.' 'Well, I've only met her a few times, so I don't really know anything about her.' 'Oh.' The paintings that got damaged were from 1968, his mother explained on TV, painted when she was a young woman living in Paris (where Eric was born).

"And how much were they worth?"

"I'm not going to comment on that. I think that's a vulgar question."

"But they were insured?"

"Yes. They were insured." And her name? Well, obviously her name was Francesca Crawford. Making Eric, Eric Crawford and Eleanor, Eleanor Crawford.

'How did she look, Francesca?' 'Slim with long features.' 'And what did she do?' In 1968 aged eighteen, she left England to go to an art school, in Paris. She was an artistically gifted kid who got swept away by a promise. That promise was the promise of Art. In the end she would be transformed.

'That was how exactly?' 'Like this…'

Responding to an advertisement, she moved out of the hotel room, first into a shared apartment. Her new flatmate was Jack, an American studying photography, a timely thing in 1968. They went to bed together, one evening, after a night in the local bar. It didn't seem such a crazy thing to do, just curiosity unfolding with freedom.

'And where?' 'Well, obviously, it was five minutes' walk from the guillotine. Art, sex, politics, and religion on the surrounding four walls.' The Storyteller tried to think of Francesca in the midst of that most revolutionary of years.

It was her teacher she actually fell for, Monsieur Bickert. A slim man of average height, with a nest of curly hair. And unfortunately, in competition for him was a wife, Celine. A young woman from an affluent family. Through gossip, she learned that Bertrand was a man who at twenty-nine years old had given up on himself, which explained why he was married. The situation seemed absurd. So, she tried to find out why. It got them into lovers' fights, which she remembered as she left her interview. She asked him once to paint her, she would do anything for him, but he flatly refused. He was castrated. 'Why?' he would always ask her. Words and words, and words, would follow, uttered to her with that straightjacketed look on his Gallic face.

When, through disinhibition, she fell pregnant, Jack helped her with the decision. Have the child, somehow, in Paris. Because she feared England. After Jack graduated there was a job for him taking pictures for an American paper. The confrontations in the streets against de Gaulle. So, he was able to pay for things.

In Stockholm's commercial district she began now to think about the paintings. Where her hands were when she painted them, around her swollen belly, at the easel by the window in her room. Bertrand continued, after official teaching hours, to instruct her. Perhaps the future was on his mind.

Twelve months later and a second child, and Jack and her friends began to think: what was the stupid English girl doing? The new baby, Sofia, with dark hair like Francesca, became the apple of Bertrand's eye. But the sweetness of it began to change when he lost his job. The scandal had reached the ears of too many people.

Changing places, in the dance that had begun between them in 1968, saw Jack move out, and Bertrand move in. To what became their own *atelier de peintre*.

One day, some months later, Francesca and Bertrand answered the door dressed in their painting finery. A French policeman stood calmly outside. '*Connaissez-vous Jack?*' he enquired. Looking at them directly.

'*Oui, oui,*' they replied. They knew Jack. 'Is Jack in trouble?'

'Jack is dead,' he said, casually. 'You can see his body, if you like.'

She fled Paris, for England.

The car stopped. Across the pavement, through the glass, the upmarket restaurant emanated a rich honeyed light. She lifted her leg. "Good evening, Madam."

"Good evening," she replied.

"I'm so sorry," said Martin, putting an arm around her, kissing her. "Tell me please, what happened?" In another country, Francesca had found herself at the wrong time, she said, in a gallery. She described to Martin the sound their feet made on the wooden floor, and the yellow paint thrown at her. And the sheets of paper printed and dashed '*Förräderi!*'

'Take the picture!' she demanded in the moment, reacting quickly to the situation. Francesca explained they had told her what the word meant, which was 'Betrayal'.

"It's a difficult time. I am sorry it happened."

"What do they want?" asked Francesca.

"They want a sort of revolution. And you're a target because it will make the news. It is something which is inevitable, I'm afraid."

"When I was being attacked, it made me feel like I was the one without power."

"I know and I'm sorry. It's because you are a painter, you see. You're now seen to represent something authentic."

"Authentic *and* a traitor?" she said. "I have to take this, I'm sorry." She answered her phone. "Yes. No, I'm all right. Yes, I'm just having dinner with Martin. I'll be at the hotel later…"

"They keep calling to check I'm okay," she said, closing it.

"Sofia?"

"She wasn't with us, thankfully."

"Where did they take you?"

"To the hospital. No one wanted to touch me. They thought I could be radioactive." She met Martin's eyes. "But if there's one thing I do know," Francesca smiled, "it's paint. That's the one thing I know. Now, let's talk about something else, shall we?" she said. They ordered and ate together. Twenty years ago, it was her first show in Sweden. Martin was a curator then and not, as he was now, a minister in the government for culture.

"And Sofia?" he asked, looking up. He remembered the teenage girl.

"She's fine," smiled Francesca, "still travelling with me. You know, she's forty now?"

"My God," he smiled.

"I know. I protect her too much," she said, and shook her head. The attraction of Martin was that Martin was a man content. He had always been, with himself and the wider world, and it hadn't changed. A serious person, who was lucky enough to be in the right place and to care about what he did.

"I can hear you thinking," he said.

"Well," said Francesca, "I was wondering if it's possible to meet them?" She held on to the idea, as she travelled back to the hotel.

"Erm, well," he said, "it's possible, I'm sure. But whether it's advisable, I don't know. You'll attract a lot of attention, you know, Francesca."

"Yes," and she knew. She sat down in front of the hotel mirror and removed her jewellery.

"What are you doing tomorrow?" asked Martin.

"Publicity," she said.

"Okay, then I will find out for you."

"Thank you," she said.

"You haven't – what's your expression – mellowed." His eyes creased.

"No. Not yet," she replied. They slipped into separate cars.

"Will I see you again?" he asked her.

"I hope so."

"Okay. Well, goodnight," he said. He closed the car door. She stood in her nightgown, beside the glass doors, absorbing the sight of the water.

4

After completing morning classes, Eric stood outside and rolled himself a cigarette. He didn't so much love smoking as the gift it afforded of solitude. He had said something to his students that he wanted to think about; carried him promptly to the spot in the courtyard outside his building where he stood on most occasions to smoke. And there, cigarette in hand, the smoke in and out of his lungs, he thought. That strange comment went like this. 'Take a blackbird,' he had said, because he had seen one scuttle over the grass that morning, 'and let it guide you,' he'd told them. He took another drag. He'd then needlessly listed its attributes – coverts, mantle – to elaborate his point, that sometimes inspiration necessitated that you consider the lives, not just of other people, but of other species. While he stood there, the bird appeared on the ground, its crest and feathers wet. "What do you want, blackbird?" he asked, but the bird peered blankly at him through yellow rings.

Absently Eric recalled that he had to go into town for Eleanor's book. The one he'd bought for her about Spain, a part of her birthday present. She was planning a trip with her friends. He finished and then squashed the cigarette. Then he went back to his office.

"Are we waiting for anyone?" he asked his students. The office doubled as his seminar room.

"Only you," remarked Tina. She gave back his keys.

"Thanks."

"Right," he said. "Has everyone read it?" He sat down and opened the pages, looking around their faces.

"Tina." He chose her first. "What did you make of it?"

"The sun and its heat represent the authoritarian power of the state," she said, as though she had rehearsed it.

"That's a grand way of looking at it. And if you had to be more specific?" he asked. "How else is it rendered?"

"The power of the state," she repeated.

"By his body," said Javid. "Fear. He knows at the end he will face justice, and probably violence."

"I agree with you," said Eric. "And the pace of the language?" he suggested. "What about that? Is that persuasive?"

Sam, one of his best students that year, then added laconically, "We're discouraged from thinking critically because the form gives us pleasure and it's pleasure more than anything that disarms criticism." They thought about what he said. "Pleasure is often mistaken for freedom," he concluded.

"That's a very sophisticated point," said Eric. "Maybe we can return to it next time? Before we pack up today, I need to remind you that we need volunteers for Open Day. I have to ask, but if you are available."

"Okay," said Javid.

"Great," said Eric.

"I'll try," said Tina.

"That's all I can ask."

The full stop armature of the Storyteller's typewriter landed to create its customary perforation. On the other side of that divide, Eric was moved to pick up the sheet of paper on which he'd brainstormed his competition entry. Eric found, on the surface of the slip, a little black circle of paper, which he lifted by pressing it with his finger. The Storyteller, also curious (but, for the moment, insufficiently), cranked out the page. He could see light emerging through those perforations but dismissed it, rolling in a fresh sheet. Eric, with his own distractions, picked up the phone.

"Hello? Hello, Rebecca. Yes." He listened. "Well, I don't mind asking. Yes. Yes. All right. I'll let you know." He put down the receiver. It stopped him for a moment. Ever since he and Madeline, that is, Eleanor's mother, had split, Rebecca had begun to rely on him for things. For answers. Today it was about her son, that is, Rebecca and her husband Joe, their youngest son, the boy Alex. He was drawing weird pictures, apparently. Lines and circles. It led Eric to salutary comments like, 'Okay', and 'I see', and 'Uh huh'. He promised that he would speak to his colleague, Barbara, who taught the developmental psychology course. And while he didn't, as such, mind, it led him to an expectation of seeming the fool.

"Barbara?" he said, about twenty minutes later, having gone to her office. "I need to ask you a question."

"Go on."

"When do children begin drawing abstract shapes?"

"Well, their first drawing is probably abstract, isn't it? It really depends on what you mean."

"Intentionally," said Eric.

"Well, I don't know. I'd have to think about it." Barbara went on moving paperwork about her desk. "Oh, and Eric?" She looked up.

"Yes?"

"Don't forget that you promised to attend that meeting with me."

"No."

———•———

On the way back to his office he spotted David, at the small courtyard. This was something which caught him off guard. He hadn't realised that David Spurling was back at the college.

"Hello, David, how are you? You're back at college?"

"Yes," said David.

"And everything's okay?"

"Yes."

"Good. It's good to have you back."

"How do I do this?" asked David, pointing at the Open Day poster.

"You just need to express an interest," said Eric. "But it's not compulsory, David. You don't have to."

"Yeah," said David. The young man looked at him.

"I have a few things I have to do, but welcome back, David." He left the boy where he stood. Then had a cigarette behind his block.

Why was he a teacher? In his office, he poured himself a coffee. Because his upbringing had disconnected him from his mother and father. He'd always been curious of boys, obviously, with parents. For him his grandparents had taken the hit. Is that why he was a teacher? So, he could spend his days observing the effect parents had on their children? God knows. Or was he out to prove that all children needed was a good teacher like him, Eric Crawford, he thought to himself, slugging the drink.

A few errands then. He had an appointment to make with Latham, 'the boss', for his annual review. And he had to check with the shop that they had Eleanor's book. Having swiftly done both he got into the burgundy car to meet her for lunch.

"I've still got to get your present," said Eric, sprinkling sugar into his coffee and dipping the spoon. "I'll pick it up after work." He lifted it to his lips.

"*No te preocupes.*" Eleanor had begun learning the language.

"No, I don't really think of her as a mother," he said, referring to Francesca.

"What do you think's going to happen?" smiled Eleanor.

"I've no idea." He didn't understand the machinations of the art world.

"I've never read that, that sort of book," he said, referring to the book Eleanor had brought with her, flat on the table. His daughter's tastes were more austere than his.

"Do you ever wonder why you exist when there are so many people?" she asked him.

"I do," he said. But it was one of those impossible questions.

"And that's why Gran knows French?" Referring to where her grandmother's damaged paintings were painted.

"Yes," said Eric.

She stretched her arms and opened her mouth to yawn.

"Happy birthday," she said.

"Thanks. Are you looking forward to the party?" he asked. Eleanor shrugged. He wasn't really looking forward to it either, but when Rebecca Lark insisted there was no option.

"Have you seen Margarita?"

"What?" he said. "No, I haven't. I think she may have gone home." Eleanor liked Margarita, the college Spanish teacher. Mainly, he thought, because of the free Spanish lessons it got her. All Margarita had wanted to do with him in quite a profound way, he found, was talk. A good skill to have as a teacher. The thought went through his mind and out again, like the roving bumble bee at their table.

"It's her mother, I think," said Eric. Explaining Margarita's whereabouts.

"I'll text her," said Eleanor.

"Do," he said. He'd begun seeing Margarita by accident. She taught the adult Spanish class at the college. Classes which were free to staff. He'd sat in to help Eleanor. They used to go out afterwards, the group. Their conversations became too – he struggled to find the word – *intense*, probably.

"I'd better go," he told Eleanor.

He ditched the pen he had been using to mark papers with and turned around to face the window. The large panes snubbing the enquiring tendril tips of the tree branches outside. The Latin name of the blackbird was *turdus murula*. He was moved to connect the bird with Margarita, since his conversation with Eleanor. Both were dark-featured and speakers of a foreign language. If that forced the point.

'I'm going to say it in a minute,' he recalled Margarita telling him. 'I'm just getting to it. But I always rehearse what I'm going to say, because English is not my first language, you understand? You have to tell yourself not to be afraid. You know?' Then she told him. 'But I read. And, well, you like to know what stories are?' She moved her hand. It was true, he did. 'And so, I will tell you,' she smiled. 'I say that our story is the problem. You have to write a new one. Can

I read you something?' Eric nodded. 'Ideas come from the powerful,' she began. 'And this restricts the shape of the future. So, we end up not having all the thoughts or living the lives we're capable of. We are blindfolded. In the future, I hope that our children,' she smiled, 'they will have ideas that function better. Not ideas, say, just of love or just God. Not even ideas of beauty,' she said. 'Because beauty is the devil. And the young,' she said, 'they're going to miss the old stories? No,' she answered. 'But we will miss them, painfully,' she laughed. 'There!' she said. 'I have explained stories to you!' Margarita was right about one thing. He had always been interested in stories. That was why he'd studied, and he now taught, English. There was a knock at the door.

"Yes?"

"I've got these for you." Miriam entered, their college administrator. She dropped the envelopes on his desk.

"Thanks," he told her. A glance at the time. He took his bag and locked the door. Then pushed the building's copper-handled external door and walked to the car.

5

The centre of town, Eric found, was a braying, shrill, whistling concatenation of sound. Okay, well, that was all right, to a point, a healthy feature of the animated city. A cordoned-off pen of metal barricades – Eric put the cigarette held between his fingers to his lips as he sat at home to think about it. He saw beneath his feet the detritus of trodden-upon paper. One carried an author's name, another a character from Shakespeare. The stuff of his career. One the name of a film club. He picked it up. This is where it got strange, which is to say that this is where it also got dangerous (as Eric found out, didn't you? Eric lifts his chin and looks up). It made it clear that the event he'd stumbled upon was no benign celebration but an organised protest. He read from the flyer a string of cultural disasters, indexed and with a demand for 'proper regulation of the most powerful thing ever invented'. And what was that? It was cinema, of course. Just like in 1968. The surprise of the police officer's hand on his shoulder encouraged a quickening of the pace, as amplified voices began screaming from handheld megaphones. The message may not have been angry, but that was how it sounded. Incongruously, Eric's movements did not speed up, however, but slowed (Eleanor's book carried limp in his fingers. Now on the dining-room table), fixated on the jousted placards. He was curious. More than that, he was fascinated. At that moment the scene before him exploded. The barriers were jumped, creating a tide of people. A woman half fell, to whom, acting on instinct, he bent to help, but he needn't have.

'Get your fucking hands off me!' she replied.

'What are you all here for?' Eric asked, taken aback by her abrupt response.

'Poetry,' she said, looking at him disdainfully; when it was that he saw blood across her teeth.

'Don't let them catch you with those,' she said, and snatched the papers away.

"Eric? Mind that cigarette."

"Oh, yes," he said, looking down at it burning. It was then, as he made his retreat, that a familiar set of words were presented to him: *'Love It Be Love'* he saw, scrawled on a placard. Eric was filled, that instant, with the sense of something unstoppable occurring. He knew he needed to watch that film. He slipped between the packed bodies, advancing as a particle in this tight city. He drove home in a state of disquiet; where he left Eleanor's book on the table, and then lit a cigarette and sat down. Why not put your culture on trial?

Finishing it, Eric climbed the staircase and undressed. Covering the wooden floorboards to the bathroom where, behind the opaque window, the sun glowed cool. He was trying to slow the pace of his mind. He knew the protestors were either right or wrong, which, put another way, meant he had to pick a side. Choose the healthiest story, he thought. A sentiment with its own power. He squeak-loosened the taps and let the water pour. Idiosyncratically he retained, on a low purposeful table, a 'Bachelor's Tumbler', as he called it, along with a short glass. Into it he tipped the contents of the tumbler, producing a trickle of rich mahogany liquid, which he put to his lips. This was for soothing's sake. With both hands he then removed his glasses, blinking as the room fell out of focus; delicately folding their insectoid arms. The bathwater lapped, and he took a towel. Domesticated. Ready then, he screwed shut the flow and plunged in a foot, then a second. Two then became four with the cheeks of his buttocks. And practical matters ensued. He dried his hands and reached out to collect the cigarette packet. He found it difficult to repress an image of the blood in the woman's mouth. He lit another cigarette. What had happened in the square? Where was the fuse? Who had lit it? His mother? There was the empirical certainty of his bathroom and that was it. He discarded the lighter and sat back against the enamel; above him the twin vapours of steam and cigarette smoke, first cautious of one another before finding amicable union. He considered what Margarita had said to him, a matter of choice between God or Love or Beauty – three categories of the same thing. He drew again on the cigarette. Were they a crime of ideas? The answer was 'Yes'. It appeared to him like that. He reached over the rim to drop the butt. He lay with his face fixed on the ceiling. History never left you alone. It was no surprise then, as he thought about it, that he had been attracted to the competition – he probably had something to say. Taking Margarita's suggestion, he wondered what would happen if you chose not to choose? Would that destroy a person? Eric blinked. Or liberate them? He slid his body beneath the water. *The end.* But nothing ended like that. Twenty minutes later he was towelling himself down, and then, downstairs in the living room, he heard Eleanor.

"Hi," said Eric.

"What's this?" said Eleanor. She took off her coat in the doorway. Eric had the television on.

"The protest," said Eric. "Did you see it?"

"Yeah, I heard about it," she said.

"I got caught up in it when I got your book."

"Sorry."

"It's not your fault," said Eric. "It was quite serious."

"Yeah. Well, I spoke to Mum and she's already at the police station." Madeline was a solicitor, and these were the sort of cases she represented. Public order offences. "Did you see what happened at the cinema?" said Eleanor.

"No," said Eric. Eleanor took the remote from his hand and changed the channel.

6

"We're standing just outside the Carlton Cinema. Yes…" The newsman listened to his earpiece for a moment. "Yes, 'hysteria' is the word that describes today's events." He consulted his notes. "Calls to emergency services were made around four o'clock. We watched several people be removed by paramedics. It may be something they've eaten. It may be something they've seen."

"Christ," said Eric. Eleanor remained silent.

"Rob," the news anchor asked the reporter, "the question on everyone's lips is, is it safe?"

"That's difficult to say, Michael. One lady I spoke to, told me 'we went to the cinema to have fun, but some people in the audience were disruptive'. Darren Orton, the cinema manager, told us 'the cinema is safe, but anyone with health concerns should visit their doctor'."

"So, not exactly clear, Rob?"

"No. Joining me from The Wednesday Group, is Adam Wright. Adam Wright, tell us why you're here today?"

"Well, look, firstly this country is just a fucking disgrace. We've been campaigning on this issue for years, emphasising the very serious consequences when you put this type of product together."

"Meaning what?"

"Music and the moving image. I mean, have we all forgotten our history?"

"You think that people going to the cinema are vulnerable?"

"Yes. I used to go, but it nearly killed me."

"How credible is that? If I said to you that cinema is harmless entertainment, what would you say?"

"I'd say you were nuts."

"What is it you think happened today?"

"People got overwhelmed like they always do."

"Okay, Adam, thank you. And we apologise to our viewers for the bad language. We are now joined in the studio by anthropologist, author and, appropriately for today, a one-time actor, Dr Andrew Philpott. Erm, Dr Philpott, what's your take on it? Should we all be afraid of the talkies?"

"Thank you again for having me on the programme. Well, I am tempted to ask a different question, actually, which is: 'how would our lives be different if we didn't watch screens?' The answer is no different at all. But let's ignore the screen and think about the image. In an important way – sorry, are you happy?"

"Please…"

"Okay. To my mind there is a direct line between organised religion and the movies."

"Does that make Adam Wright, from The Wednesday Group, right?"

"Well, yes, but if anything, I would emphasise the benefit, rather than the harm. Everyone gets psychological comfort from seeing themselves inside a plot. Plot, in a sense, keeps us safe. Many centuries ago, when the majority of us were illiterate, we consumed just one story. The story of Christ. That was in the form of comic book-like frescos. These were the frames through which we understood the plot of life. Over time, the Church's influence has naturally weakened, and literacy has spread. So that the power of the image, without being diminished, diversified, giving rise to different sources. Our minds diversified with them. Paintings, plays, expanded with democratic force, until eventually we come to the moving image. But to be clear about it, at no point in this story does our relationship with the image change. I would like to say that these early frescos were in every sense the cinema of their time. If I put it this way, explicit Church doctrine has been removed from our images, but images are still our religion."

"Sounds like there's good reason to be alarmed then?"

"I think we're safe for now."

"Dr Philpott, thank you. Rob, I think we're going back to you."

"'I thought it was a prank, you know a promotion', said Diana Smart. 'Local theatre crowd reports dangerously high levels of stimulation', that's how the BBC are reporting it. 'People must understand that today's cinema is an incredibly sophisticated blend of fact and fiction', that's from Media Now. 'Yes, yes, yes', says Mark Stevens, from Colchester, 'it is *de facto* a public health issue'. 'Commonly associated', says GP Rose Gower, 'with sleeplessness and depression'. Sarah McMaster, aged eleven, says, 'There was lots of screaming, and I didn't like it'. Back to you."

"I met some of The Wednesday Group outside the hospital," said Eric. "When I went there for David." He looked at Eleanor.

"Yeah," said Eleanor.

"Do you know who they are?"

"Just students, I think. Don't forget, Dad, you're supposed to be getting ready."

"Yes," said Eric. He still had The Wednesday Group's flyer in his drawer.

"It is Wednesday today, isn't it?" said Eric.

"Yeah," said Eleanor. "It's their thing, Dad."

Eric climbed the stairs, under the illusion of getting himself ready, and typed into his computer: 'The Wednesday Group'. The search gave him their website. Today's date was there, under 'Events', and looking back in the calendar the day at the hospital with David. The dates also went forward into the future. Each one of them was a Wednesday.

"Dad," knocked Eleanor.

"Yes. I'm getting ready," he said.

7

Eric slipped his arms into a shirt, each foot a shoe. Plucking an unscrutinised bottle from the kitchen. The Larks lived so close that their buzzer was ringing beneath his finger before his feet met their pillared gate, even before he got into his car and ignited the engine. The fact, of course, was that it didn't really matter.

"We thought you weren't coming," said Joe, propping his arm on the door frame. "Come in." Eric followed. "Here he is. The young people are in the garden," added Joe.

"If it isn't father of the year. Hello, Eric," said Rebecca, and she stood up to embrace him. "Do you want a drink?"

"So, what did you get her?" asked Joe. "Another copy of the dictionary?" he laughed.

"When did you start?" Eric asked.

"Seven," said Rebecca.

———•———

What about Rebecca? With each punch of the Storyteller's typewriter another brick. She had intended to complete her postgraduate studies and then go on to teach, like Eric. But post-partum depression had scotched it. She couldn't put in the work; her mind wasn't there. We look at her and we describe: behind the smile and the attention, and all the food she has prepared, there is still this devastation. She had been ignoring the signs, stress, anxiety, exhaustion, depression. They were all offered up – "Yes there's more!" she smiles. But in catching our interest noticeably tightens. We know that if she ever lost her smile, then she'd be a goner. Well, that was all right, wasn't it, no harm done. You just had to rest for a while and 'get back on the horse', that's what you did, wasn't it? When life threw things at you? She did try, but a previous vice-like grasp of the facts, she discovered, and vision that was normally gimlet clear, had gone. In its place an awful blur, that dreadful abnegating blur was in control. Doctor's appointments and referrals gave her a diagnosis and a prescription, but not a solution. That was why when Eric looked at her sometimes it carried with it the shock of electricity. It reminded her of who she had wanted to be.

"Eric, have you got anything to tell us?" asked Rebecca. Her eyes passed from Joe to Eric. "You've always got something to entertain us with." So, Eric proceeded to tell them about the protest, and the girl with the bloodied mouth, ("You've always been a charmer," said Joe, and laughed) and then afterwards about David. It just came out. It didn't take Eric long to realise that with these anecdotes he was working things out.

"Well," said Rebecca. "That's all very strange."

"He one of your students?" asked Joe of David. Then without waiting for the answer, "You have to be careful.

Whatever it is you're teaching them." It gave Eric a shudder of double-quick sensory memory.

'Why didn't you stop?' Eric had asked David.

'I hit the wrong pedal.'

'You were driving pretty fast.'

'I suppose…' The monitor on David's chest bleeped and fell silent. It was 'going like the clappers', the doctor had told them. Some sort of panic attack. But David looked very peaceful now.

'Do you want me to call your parents?' Eric asked.

'No,' answered David. Then the nurse interrupted them with a misapprehension. 'Are you Dad?' she asked Eric.

'No. I'm a teacher from his college. Do you want me to wait?'

'You're best to speak to the charge nurse.' Eric left the protection of the curtain, where he found a woman waiting similarly to be told what to do, so he joined her.

'He's your son?' she asked, inclining her head to the curtain behind them.

'No. He's a student. I'm a teacher,' said Eric.

'I'm here for my son,' she smiled. 'The idiot. You must have something better to do than spend your time chasing after your students?' She got up from the chair. 'If they come back, would you mind telling them I haven't left? I just have to make a call.' She opened her small bag, searched for a moment and then gave Eric her card. 'Just in case,' she said.

'No,' said Eric. He took the card from her. When he read it, the name was shot with a significance he couldn't have imagined. It seemed like an impossible name: Gloria Bell. A character name. He thought of the production he'd set to write, while he turned the card between his fingers.

The ward received briskly a masked doctor leading a police officer. *Coming for David?* Eric thought. The police officer carried a nondescript box. Eric's eyes followed them. It struck Eric, something else, watching this, that it should begin at the hospital. Where all things began.

'Do a lot of people come in, like him?' Eric asked the charge nurse about David.

'You mean in similar circumstances? We're all human, aren't we?' he replied. 'Just your phone number.' Eric gave the number and left to smoke a cigarette outside.

"We heard something about this, didn't we?" said Joe. "That they're admitting lots of people these days with 'sensitivities'," he said. "What on earth that means." Joe tipped the bottle to his mouth. It sharpened the sense Eric had that they all knew, really, the point young people were making. And they had to wake up to it. *What happened then outside the hospital. How he ended up with that flyer.* It was a good example, so he went on with it.

Cigarette in hand, two young men hastily, made up as clowns, dressed in 'A'-shaped sandwich boards, appeared by the entrance. A kid's educational event, he thought. One clown taller than the other. On the front of the sandwich boards, which were printed identically, were eyes, ears, and noses, but dramatically oversized.

'Cover your face, you idiot!' The mini drama began.

'You cover your face!' the other snapped. A melee ensued in which each attempted to cover the images on the other's sandwich board with their hands, which, being the only element ordinary in size, were too small. This drawback halted the duo temporarily.

'You know what…' smaller clown said.

'What?' said taller. From a box the smaller clown pulled out a handful of rubber masks, which he played with, for a moment, like balloons.

'Why don't we put these on?' They looked at them. In

doing so they tempted the audience. That audience being today an English teacher called Eric.

'That's better.'

'Much better.' They stood for a moment. When Smaller looked at Taller, he was standing there petrified, covering his eyes.

'What's the matter?'

'Him.' He elbowed towards Eric. 'He's looking at me funny.'

'He's not wearing a mask,' said Smaller, in a 'what do you expect' sort of manner.

'You promise he will?'

'Yes, of course. I promise. It's easy, isn't it, for people to look at one another and jump to the wrong conclusions.' Taller nodded. 'That's because faces are stories too,' said Smaller, sagely.

'Is it safe now?'

'Yes.'

'Oh, good.' Taller one uncovered his eyes.

'You see. It's the senses. If we manage them better, then you don't need to be afraid.' The pair then broke from character.

'We're The Wednesday Group. And we're spreading awareness that our human senses are a part of the impending catastrophe. You got to "look right to get right",' he said. 'You should check it out right here.' He pointed at their flyer. 'This week eyes and faces. Last week we did ears for hearing and noses for smell.' Eric took a flyer.

'You should tell people about us,' said Taller.

"It's no surprise then, is it?" said Joe. "With lunatics like that about."

After the clowns' performance, Eric had bought himself a coffee. He took out a pen and looked at the flyer.

On its edge he wrote, without pause, 'We cut you open with a comma and cauterise you with a question mark.' He had no idea where those words came from. But they made plain what his new sense of purpose was.

'Go on, pick a colour.' The masks the clowns offered were three colours. Red, green and yellow. The one he had chosen was yellow. He wondered to himself, *was it as easy to choose a story?*

"You know," interrupted Joe, "Madeline's here."

8

On the porch by the front door Rebecca took the lighter.

"So how is it?" she said. "Is anyone else leaving?" It was true, considered Eric, that of late there had been a recent increase in the number of staff departing the college. It was due to politics.

"One or two," confirmed Eric.

"Why?"

"Institutions change."

"But you still like it?" asked Rebecca.

"Yes," Eric agreed.

"That's something." Brian Catchpole left. But he had retired. And Eric's friend, Georgina, she'd gone for... well, he didn't know why. He was hoping he would find out tonight. He'd asked Georgina out for a drink so he would have a reason to leave the party. Certainly, if not outright exodus there was undoubtedly unease in the teacher body. When young people showed signs of rebellion, it didn't take long for scrutiny to fall on their teachers.

"What does Madeline think?" asked Rebecca.

"About what?"

"I don't know. Your job? You can just put it there," she said, tapping ash onto the earth. "You'll tell me, won't you?" she said, folding her arms.

"Yes," he said and nodded. He hadn't been thinking of leaving. He liked the school, and he liked his students. But Rebecca had, for reasons unclear, latched onto the idea. Maybe she didn't want it to be a good job.

"Did something happen the other day?" He watched Rebecca's face.

"Brotherly jealousy," she said, somewhat fiercely. "Alex was awestruck, I think. The only female body he's ever seen is mine. And it's quite different. I asked Eleanor and Richard to be careful about their behaviour. That's all. I hope you don't mind."

"No. They should be careful."

"Good." Rebecca nodded. "It doesn't need to be a thing." Their ears drew them to the window. That sound they could hear was Madeline's laughter.

"She seems happy," said Rebecca.

"Yes," agreed Eric. Rebecca was right. Madeline did seem happy.

Rebecca put the base of the cigarette to her lips.

"I shouldn't be smoking," she said. Then it was Richard's turn.

"Do we have any more beer?" he asked.

"Check the shed or your father."

Eric looked at Richard, while Richard looked at Eric.

"Happy birthday, Eric."

"Thanks," said Eric.

The smoke from their cigarettes rose into the night air.

"We still think its improbable that you and Eleanor were born on the same day. It makes you think there's some sort of plan. How much longer do we have?" she asked. He thought for a moment about how much their kids had grown, but that thinking, just like the smoke, drifted.

"I told Joe you would take him," said Rebecca. She wanted Eric to show Richard the college. He had exams to re-sit. "It would be a relief. To have him on his way. Otherwise, I'm afraid he'll fester. You've seen what can happen. This should be a summer thing," she said, looking at the glowing ember, and clenched her folded arms. "Shall we go inside?"

They entered the house to Joe telling Madeline, "They say that confronting your problems makes it easier, but it doesn't seem that way to me." He peeled the cap from another bottle and then saw his wife. "You all right?" Eric took the moment of awkwardness to go up to the bathroom. Holding himself, he imagined each of the adults foreheads adorned with post-it notes that named their personal issues in a psychological parlour game. He rinsed his hands and looked at himself in the mirror. The man he saw was a little spiral-eyed. The inauguration process of his forty-third year. Outside the bathroom he came across Rebecca's youngest son, Alex, who was sitting on the floor in his bedroom, drawing.

"Are you enjoying the party?" The boy looked up and shrugged. "You don't like parties?" said Eric. "Well, this looks more constructive." Eric sat down. "I can see you really like drawing. How often do you draw?" The boy thought to himself before answering.

"Every day," he said.

"I imagine school gets in the way."

"Yeah." He nodded.

"It doesn't change when you get older, I'm afraid." Eric picked up an image. "I've still got your other picture," he said. "The one you gave me of the lines and circles."

"The one in space."

"Yes. I like it," said Eric. "It's very interesting. It makes me think." The boy continued to propel the coloured pen across the page.

"Do you get a lot of praise from your teachers at school for drawing?" The boy nodded.

"You should keep doing it." There was a pause.

"It's your birthday today, isn't it?" said the boy.

"Yes. And Eleanor's."

"That's weird."

"Being born on the same day?" asked Eric. The boy nodded.

"You can have this one." Alex passed him the sheet of paper. Eric took it from the boy's hand. It was similar to the one he'd been given before.

"What do you think about when you're drawing?"

"Nothing in particular." Eric nodded. The pair were then interrupted by Rebecca.

"So, this is where you are," said Rebecca. "What do you think, professor? You'd spend all summer up here if you could, wouldn't you?" Alex nodded. She stood over them holding a glass.

"See. I told you. And you're bending Eric's ear. He's learning to play the guitar too. Aren't you?" Rebecca sipped from the glass. "I need the loo." She stroked the hair on Alex's head and then put her hand on Eric's shoulder. He left the boy and went downstairs, where he found Eleanor on the garden patio.

"Are you having a good time?"

"Yeah." She shrugged neutrally.

"Is your mum okay?"

"I think so." They turned their heads in the direction of inside.

"Where are you going afterwards?"

"I don't know. A bar in town, I think. You can come," said Eleanor.

"Oh, no." Eric shook his head and smiled. "Have you got enough money?"

"Yes, Dad." She frowned. "It's my birthday."

"That's true."

"I think Richard wants to talk to you," said Eleanor. "He won't tell me what it's about."

"I think it's about college," said Eric. Eleanor shrugged. The kids partied while their parents got drunk. He found himself wondering about Rebecca and her iceberg. At least he and Madeline were okay, he thought.

Time then passed rapidly.

"Are you ready?" Madeline asked.

"Yes." He buried his cigarette.

———•———

Eric and Madeline left the house together.

"Are you going home?" said Madeline.

"No. I'm meeting a friend, I think." He fished for his phone.

Madeline took out her keys. "Okay. Well, I'll see you then." She smiled. "We should probably talk about…"

"Yes." What Eleanor was going to do.

"Goodnight."

He sat in the car and watched Madeline leave the space at the kerb. Then he followed her taillights, wipers tracing back and forth. The feeling of being her jilted lover came over him. The basis for a habit of recollection, which festered until you felt the way he did; or sometimes did, let's be honest. Setting keys on the loose surface of the hallway table, while the streetlight spread over the surface of the carpet, he slumped in the chair. He shouldn't have driven, he felt, fingers looking for tobacco. The boy's picture joined the other one resting on the table. Only then, did Eric layer the paper trench, poke out his tongue and lick the gummed edge, and wheel and light the touch paper; standing with his spine pressed against the jutting frame of the sliding door, gazing up into the black sky. For the first time, you had the inspiration of a stretch of sea orbiting the moon, and you thought about how it might look, like a corona. Eric smoked. It was too good an idea. When he went back inside, Eric tore off a piece of paper and drew it. More alert now. The earth one circle, the moon another, and traced with the pen a figure of eight encompassing them both. He knew straight away that he'd been given another piece of the production. On what terms would a boy go to the moon? In a river? On an ocean? He thought about his daughter on her nineteenth birthday.

Speaking to him through their unacknowledged portal, the Storyteller told him, "We'll come back to it, Eric. Who we're going to send around the moon." The Storyteller looked down at the machine.

As for Eric, he pondered. Well, okay. Look. Let's be honest about it. This was the contract. Eric stood, gazing up into the dark sky; the Storyteller bent over the typewriter and the trapped page.

"You had to exist for me, Eric," the Storyteller told him, and Eric listened. "You remember, I hope, as a boy that you were fascinated by words. It's why you wanted to become an English teacher. I can tell you now, Eric, that you and

I are made of words. I think you probably know that and understand it better than I do. This is my last book and it's about you, Eric. Because your premise, what is it?"

"A city in need of a story," said Eric.

"Yes. That's my premise too. Let's begin by asking ourselves an elemental question. Eric, what notions would you be free of if you could?"

"Obviously illusions," said Eric, watching the stars twinkle.

"For example?"

"Destiny. God," said Eric. "And fictitious and deleterious notions that cloud our way of life."

"I see," the Storyteller smiled. "And how would we do it?"

"Well, new stories start with children. They always have," said Eric. "So, I'd start with them," Eric said. "Just like at the college."

"I see," said the Storyteller. "I think the minds we can actually change," he offered Eric, "are the minds of children, before their teenage years. What do you think?"

"You're probably right," said Eric.

"What would it take to completely transform the way a child sees the world?" asked the Storyteller. Eric thought about it. "Isn't this a transformed child, Eric, the sort of child who would tell *our* story?"

"Yes." Eric nodded. He finished his cigarette and slid the door closed.

9

Madeline got home. In the kitchen she poured herself a glass of wine. The Larks were Eric's friends, no matter how long they had known each other. It didn't bother her anymore, and in fact she preferred it that way. She squinted and swallowed. She put the cold glass to her lips and tucked her legs beneath her. With her other hand she sent Eleanor a text telling her to enjoy her night. It was true that other people thought it strange, even immoral, for a daughter not to live with her mother. But circumstances didn't always fall into preferred order; it was what worked. She ran her thumb across the screen. No amount of stigma or shaming was going to alter the fact. Madeline switched on the lamp and took out her laptop. She had about as many cases at the moment as she could handle. She finished the glass and settled it. She had court tomorrow and couldn't allow herself to drink heavily. She climbed the stairs to the bathroom, placing herself beneath the water. A bath any day of the week, but on Friday it was heaven. After that to bed in the adjacent room. She answered some texts before enjoying the vibrator she kept in her wardrobe drawer.

———•———

Eric sat in the living room, in front of the TV, but with the TV off. He flattened Alex's picture and traced the circles. So, the protagonist was a child. Localising the 'matter at hand' gave him a touch of assurance. He looked at his watch. There was still, however, that final appointment. So, he fetched his coat, patted pockets, fastened buttons and shoed it again outside down the steps. Brown leaves, which fell from the trees lining the street, littered the steps, as they did every year, decaying on the pavement and producing the strong sweet smell that he rather liked. That moment, it was raining. It seemed to be raining a lot. He held tightly to the inside of his coat, jogged to skirt the traffic, flashed a ticket and got aboard. Where he sat, he wiped, with the sleeve of his coat, the condensation from the window to get a clearer view of the street. The sloshing, sloshing sound of tyres through water. Now it was the people who were like leaves, they covered the street. He made his way to the bar on the corner. Where he sat, waiting, with his arm beside a throaty coffee machine, sipping a pint of lager. He would have to think about a venue, he thought. The obvious solution, and his distinct advantage, was the drama department at the college. He should get the students involved. He took another gentle sip and swallowed, placing the glass back carefully on the coaster.

Georgina, when she arrived, was a vision that cut a swath through the crowded bar.

"It is today, isn't it?" She stopped beside him, undoing the belt around her coat.

"Yes."

"I was a bit surprised to get your message. I thought you might be drunk."

"What would you like? I'll get it," said Eric.

"Cheers," she said.

"A little tutoring," she explained when she had sat down. That was what she was doing. "Look. Do we have to get into that? Latham was a bit weird about it and if I was paranoid, I might think you were a stooge."

"I'm just interested," smiled Eric. "I promise."

"All right then. Cheers." Her drink arrived. "Why are you thinking of leaving as well? If the loyalists are giving up…" She took a gulp from the pint.

They took a table, eventually, by the window. Outside it a monochrome street, wet and shimmering.

"Here," said Georgina. She put a five-pound note in Eric's hand.

"It's all right."

"I'd like to. Please," she said. Eric got up and returned. "So?"

"Yes," said Georgina, her eyes narrowing.

"You said you were working on a project."

"Did I?" she demurred. "This will sound a bit odd. And I expect people to look at me like that. But when I saw it, the competition email, I thought to myself, there'll never be a better reason to leave. So, you can tell Latham that's the reason. It was their own fault. I've got post-trauma-playwright-disorder." Eric looked at her. It was to her credit that she was so direct. He stood outside with his shoulder pitched against the wall. Was that why so many people were leaving? To write plays. He put it to his lips. He decided he was not going to talk about it. "But we should know what's in your first draft, don't you think, Eric?"

"I've not decided yet," said Eric, squinting.

"But won't it be about that boy? And won't it have Gloria Bell in it? And won't it be about the future?" suggested the Storyteller.

Act 1, Scene 1: The Hospital

To the right, dominating the stage, a plush living room. Left, the house's front door. Two characters, both policemen, approach.

"Can you hold this?" *The one officer hands the box to the other.*

"Mrs Bell?" *The intercom bleeps.*

"It's Miss Bell." *Gloria stands on the other side of the door.*

"Oh, I'm sorry. Miss Bell, we need to speak with you, if you have a moment." *The door opens. Gloria appears, looking beautiful.*

"What is this about?" *She looks at them and then at the watch on her wrist.*

"We would like to talk to you about your son."

"Benjamin?"

"Yes."

"I haven't seen him," *she says.*

"That's what we wanted to talk to you about."

"You'd better come in." *She leads the two officers into the sitting room.*

"I'm sorry, but I have an appointment to keep, so this will have to be quick. Is he all right?"

"We've received a phone call..."

"Oh. About what?"

"Your son."

"Well, I've not heard anything from him, but I am sure

he's all right."

"We have a responsibility in the present climate to take reports of altered behaviour very seriously," *he begins.*

"What do you mean?"

"Mrs Bell, I am sure you've seen on TV, stories of altered behaviour in young people. They've become very sensitive, you see."

"Yes, of course, but what does that have to do with Benjamin? I don't think Benjamin is the sort to be involved in anything like that."

"When did you last see your son?"

"A few weeks ago, we had lunch."

"He doesn't live here?"

"No."

"With his father?"

"No, we don't see his father. Benjamin has his own place."

"While we're here we would like to give you an item of protective equipment." *The officer opens the box.* "We recommend that you wear this in public. Or when you meet new people. We're not here to alarm you, but there has been an increase in violence, particularly against women, and the mask has proven to be very effective."

"Why would I wear that?"

"Well, it's your decision, Mrs Bell, but we would recommend that you wore it in public."

"Excuse me," *she says. She sits with the phone against her ear.*

Gloria turns directly to face the audience:

"When I think about Benjamin, I can't bear to remember the promising young man. The athlete on sports days. The son who inherited my good looks. The son who was taller than all the other boys, whose balls dropped earlier than the other boys. All that early promise, gone."

Lights out. The sound of a police siren. On our return Gloria stands dressed immaculately in front of the hospital reception:

"I'm here to see my son. Benjamin Bell," *she says.*

"One moment." *The woman types his name.* "I'll be just a second." *Gloria waits.* "You'll need to be by station 'D'; the doctor will take you to him." *She points.*

Downstage there is a dialogue between a boy and a doctor. The doctor is explaining how they are treating his mother:

"It's important that we run some tests to find out what's wrong with your mother." *The boy looks up at the doctor.* "We need to take her into another room. But my colleague will look after you, okay? You'll be able to see her as soon as we've finished." *The boy is circumspect and says nothing.*

"Mrs Bell? If you'd like to come this way."

We revolve on a carousel, patient to patient until we reach Gloria's son, Benjamin — tracking in the process the medical charts at the foot of each patient's bed. Each labelled with a cultural diagnosis, like, for example, 'A favourite book', 'A favourite song', 'A favourite colour', in bold black letters. When we arrive at Benjamin's bed we see his face is a patchwork of red and purple, and his left eye is swollen shut — with the appearance of an inflated balloon:

"You can come closer." *The doctor beckons. Benjamin blinks his one blinkable eye.*

"Benjamin?" *she asks.*

"He's taken quite a beating, but no lasting damage. It's only this eye we're worried about."

"How did this happen?" *Gloria asks.*

"He was trying to buy videos."

"I'm sorry?"

"Video tapes," *the doctor repeats.*

"Why videotapes?" *she asks.*

"A lot of people find themselves today dependant on videotapes."

An ill-timed phone call interrupts:

"I'm sorry, Doctor. I have an appointment. Is there anything he needs? Benjamin, is there anything you need?"

"He'll be well looked after."

The carousel spins again. When it stops, Gloria is there at the Grande Hotel:

"This way." *The maitre d' swiftly escorts her. The man she is to meet sits sprawled over the chair.*

"Sir, your guest."

"You're late," *he says, pulling a bottle out of the ice. He proceeds to fill his own glass. He looks at Gloria.* "You're very pretty. I thought you'd be, well..." *He smiles. Gloria removes her coat and sits down.*

"I'm sorry to be late."

"No... problem." *He waves it away.* "Time to kill." *Over the course of many years Gloria has learned how to move.*

"I've already ordered... I apologise," *he says.*

"Oh. Don't worry." *She quickly reads the menu.*

"The bream is good. But have whatever you like." *The sight of Gloria. He smiles in disbelief. Like other women, Gloria had learned to divide these appointments into careful milestones, holding back her most devastating weapon. The girls had read an article Catrina had shared with them, developing what they already knew from experience. That men overlooked subtle facial cues in favour of an on/off responsiveness to a smile. In application the principle held power by being both simple and subtle. Getting everything right, the introduction, the pitch of chest, the touch of hair (or temple), the gamut of body language, was threaded together by the reward. That's how you took control. With a smile.*

"Do you know this hotel?" *he asks, pricking an olive and popping it in mouth.*

Gloria nods. "Yes."

"I thought you would."

"How long have you been staying?" *Gloria asks. Talking is the first phase. It will stop. That is why in their team they stipulate the ordering of food. Clients think it's a cheek, but it's not.*

"Umm, three weeks now. Business."

"I'll have the sea bream, thank you," *says Gloria when the waiter comes.*

"Madame, a fantastic choice." *Gloria relinquishes the menu and sets herself again. Everything she does, you have to understand, matters. The speed at which she moves, how often she blinks, how she holds the stem of her glass, the knife and fork in her hand. It is taken for granted, when as a woman you look like Gloria, that there is a manifest perversity in everything. That is why they hire her.*

"Have you come far?" *Gloria asks. That's two questions.*

He shakes his head "No. London. I live in London. You? Do you live here?"

"Yes."

"With family?"

"No." *Gloria tips the glass toward her mouth.*

"I advise companies in financial difficulty. I'm here for

a plastics company." *First unsolicited comment.* "They pay too much for their materials. It's competitive." *The second.*

Their food arrives. He takes a knife and fork and slices the fish.

"This is a bit awkward," *he leans in and whispers,* "but I have a meeting with the partners later, so I was wondering if we could skip dessert." *This is an obvious lie. He takes Gloria to a separate room for the occasion. The anonymous room, which is another stipulation. They undress and make the transaction frantically, and then Gloria dresses and leaves. Outside the hotel her hair catches the cold sea breeze, before she retraces via a network of tight narrow streets the route back to the car. The city nightlife redefined by the beat of her shoes. En route, Catrina calls.*

"Hi, Catrina. No, I was working. Why? All right. Okay. I'm on my way home. No, no he was fine," *she says,* "the usual." *She is confused. Gloria drops her phone back into her bag. Here it comes. Coming right up for you, Gloria. The professional's misfortune. What the women had come to call a hyena. And he says to her:*

"So, you're free tonight? Me mates. We overheard. From our table." *He looks back at the table outside the bar.* "I told them what you were."

"Is she a skank?"

"No," *he replies.* "How much is it for us?" *He blinks something from his eye.* "We're good lads. I promise."

At that moment, incidentally, the owner of the bar, which is called Umberto's, stands no distance away collecting glasses, sinking one methodically inside another.

"Have you got this?" *shouts one of the boys.* "Come on, love, we're nice enough lads. We just want to go out with a…" *They laugh.*

"It's Ann? Right?" *says the owner.* "A couple of weeks ago, you were here? One of our waitresses left yesterday, if you still want the work. I can go over the details?"

"Do you mind, mate? We're doing some business."

"I do, actually… Wipe it off, your makeup, and then leave," *he tells her.* "They won't notice. Here on the side," *he points. He leaves Gloria in the kitchen, which is tiled and fashioned from stainless steel, spotless like an operating theatre. She takes a wet tissue from the packet and strokes her face, removing makeup and mascara. She could tie her hair back. Why not? While checking her phone, her fingers catch the rubber mask. She removes it, unfolds it, looks at it. Perfectly smooth. It's cold to the touch. She puts it on. She pulls the straps tight and fastens it at the back with a snap of the clip. She then looks at herself.*

The rotation of the turntable brings us back to Benjamin for the culmination of the scene.

Through that one blinkable eye he watches, behind a wall of glass, a parade of children. The process, he recognises, is – one by one – an evacuation like Noah's Ark. The parent is separated, and they go left, while the child is escorted right. Sometimes an adverse reaction, screams, but the result is always the same. It's part of it. If it weren't for the craving eating at Benjamin for something to watch, he might speak up, shout. But, of course, he doesn't.

END of Act 1, Scene 1

10

"I'm upstairs," replied Eric. He listened to the front door close and Eleanor's feet climb the stairs. Eric stopped typing.

"We have a guest," said Eleanor, slightly out of breath. "I invited Mum to watch the film."

"Okay."

"Is that all right, Dad?"

"Of course it is. She all right?" he asked.

"Yeah. I just thought," said Eleanor.

"Yes," said Eric.

"You're in shock?"

"No. I'm not in shock," he said defensively. Eleanor eyed her dad. She smiled and went downstairs. He looked over his draft, and then joined them.

"Mum's put the oven on."

"Great."

"There you are." Eleanor handed him a mug of tea.

"Thanks. I don't normally get this service," said Eric.

"I hope I'm not interrupting your evening," said Madeline.

"No," said Eric.

"Mum says the house looks the same. We think you should redecorate, Dad."

"And you'll pay for that, will you?"

"What's the film about?" asked Madeline, removing her coat.

"We saw it on the news. The people who damaged Gran's paintings watched it," said Eleanor.

"They made it sound like it was the cause," said Eric, knowing that it sounded a bit ridiculous. "So, we thought we'd see it." Eric sipped his drink. "As research."

"I see," said Madeline. They sat down in the living room and Eleanor read out the plot.

"Okay. A soldier leaves behind his fiancée to go and fight in a war. She doesn't know if he'll ever return. Pretty standard."

"Well…" said Madeline.

After watching it Eric, you thought, didn't you, in a glossy sort of way, that it was well done.

"Yes." The interesting part being that discussion about the merits of war. Because they made it sound, despite the predictable dialogue, that instead they were debating love. Madeline glanced at you a few times, didn't she? You thought it was disbelief or belief, either of them. Both of them triggered your nerves.

Eleanor switched off the television.

"Well, we won't be watching that again."

"It was all right," said Madeline. "But I don't think it explains why they vandalised your mother's exhibition."

"No, it doesn't explain it. It was just strange to me that they were talking about it," said Eric.

"Love can make people do strange things," said Madeline. "And people do things for strange reasons."

"This terrorist attack was sponsored by Coca-Cola," said Eleanor, getting up to fetch a drink.

"I have this case," said Madeline. Eric and Eleanor were used to those words. "A young man, in his early thirties. Married with a young daughter —"

"Is this the weirdo case?" asked Eleanor.

"Yes. Although we don't call it that," Madeline smiled. "He's a letting agent and every lunch time he goes out to watch this woman who works in the accounting office down the road. This woman is in her early forties, married with children. The two of them have never met. He's never made threats. He's never approached her, spoken to her or even tried. Women know that men stare at them, sometimes. The question is whether this man should be prosecuted for it. I'm defending him, I should say."

"But don't you think if he was given the chance?" said Eric.

"Well, possibly. But I don't actually think this is that case," said Madeline. "He doesn't want to confront her. That's not what this is about. His wife, bless her, says, she knows it's a part of his fantasy world."

"He's a weirdo," said Eleanor.

"Eleanor's not convinced, but I'll do my best," said Madeline. She checked her watch. "I think I should be going," she said. "Now I've subjected you to that."

―――•―――

"Thank you," she told Eric at the door. "I needed a night off."

"You're welcome," said Eric.

"I know," she said. "But I don't like to… you know. Rock the boat."

"You're not," he said. "And… you're all right?"

"Yes," said Madeline and smiled. "Why do you ask?"

"I was just asking," said Eric. "Eleanor tells me you're defending some of those protestors."

"Yes. We just want the courts to record it for what it really is. The right to protest."

"Night, Mum," said Eleanor.

"Night," she said. Eric and Eleanor watched Madeline get into her car. And then waved back as she drove away.

"It was nice to see Mum," said Eleanor.

"Yes," Eric agreed. He shut the door.

11

That evening, just as Madeline's car passed on the road below, Richard sat beside the cycle track with his friend, Darrell, drinking.

"That guy," said Richard, explaining it to Darrell, "was Eleanor's dad. And that woman, the one with dark hair, was her mother." He was answering questions prompted by the party.

"Right," said Darrell. Darrell was his closest friend, and he was off to university.

"Well, are you?" asked Darrell.

"Am I what?"

"Are the both of you?" He inclined his head. "You know."

"Yeah," said Richard.

"Cool," said Darrell. And then, "You know that kid, David, was at the party too?"

"No," said Richard. They all knew about the incident by now. Their peers seemed to agree that it wasn't all that surprising that Spurling would do something like that.

"You didn't invite him?"

"No," said Richard, "why would I?" He took a slug of beer.

"That's what I thought. So, why do you think he came when he wasn't invited?"

"How do I know?"

"What's her dad like?" said Darrell, returning to Eleanor.

"He's nice." He told Darrell about Eleanor's family. The famous grandmother.

"He's doing that play thing," said Richard. "They're going to show it at the college. They're more sorted than my parents, anyway." Richard told Darrell that his parents weren't earning enough money. But there was nothing he could do about it.

"Mine are like that," said Darrell. Which Richard knew wasn't true.

They pushed their bikes through the gates and then carried them to the cycle track.

"You pursue me," said Richard, and set off.

And then afterwards they bought beer.

"I wish they'd just sort it out." Richard took a mouthful, which frothed at the back of his throat.

"You're staying with Eleanor?"

Richard shrugged. What did he like about Eleanor? That she was smart, that she was tall, that they were young.

"Yeah," he said. 'Probably'. Richard drank the last of the can and squashed it. Then he cracked open another and checked it against the side of the one Darrell held out, and then lay back on the grass. He supposed he could sell drugs, like Vincent. But basically, he'd be better off getting a normal job.

Richard looked at the time.

"I gotta go." He stood up and brushed his jeans. "When is it you leave?" Richard asked.

"September," said Darrell.

"Okay, cool," said Richard. They picked up their bikes and cycled home. Richard locked up his bike under the shelter. The lights were off inside. He drank a glass of water, then climbed the stairs and turned on the small TV in his room. He listened to familiar words in an unfamiliar context: "Davenport College…"

12

Her father came into her room. His hands in his pockets and his long face longer than usual.

"You all right, Dad?" Eleanor asked.

He took a hand and rubbed the back of his neck.

"There's been an explosion at the college. Jim's been trying to contact me. I just spoke to him. I can't go to work tomorrow. It's all over the news."

"Fuck. What are you going to do?"

"Wait, I suppose. He had to give my number to the police. They want to talk to me."

"Why?"

"Procedure, I suppose."

"So, basically, someone blew up your building?"

"Yeah. It looks like that."

"Why?"

"I don't know."

"Was there anyone inside?"

"No. I don't think so."

"Fuck," repeated Eleanor.

"I know," said Eric. They went downstairs and switched on the TV.

"The police and emergency services were called tonight to a large explosion at Davenport College. No explanation has been given so far. What we do know is that the building that lies in rubble behind me used to be the English department."

The phone rang and Eric quickly picked it up.

"Eric?" she said.

"Yes, we see it," he replied.

"That's your building."

"Yes. You're right." He found it rather difficult to think of anything to say.

"Is Eleanor all right?"

"Yes, I think so. She's here next to me. Your mum wants to know if you're all right." He handed her the phone.

He could have been there, in principle, he reflected, and no doubt would have been killed. Quite a prospect to consider, being flattened by your building. There was little for any of them to do, except to stare at the scenes being repeated on TV.

At the end of a long evening punctuated with phone calls they finally went to bed.

"I hope you sleep all right," said Eric, standing by her door.

"You too, Dad," she said.

"If you need anything…" he began.

"Thanks, Dad."

"Okay. Goodnight." He closed the door to Eleanor's room. Then he brushed his teeth, before slipping into bed and turning off the light. There he lay awake in an effort to process what was happening.

'Look I'll call you tomorrow with an update,' he'd listened to Jim. 'Nobody knows what's going on.'

The next day the police officer invited him to sit down.

"Tea?"

"No thanks," said Eric.

"All right. Are you aware of any reason why your building would be targeted?"

"No," Eric replied. It was a surreal experience, cops on campus. He hadn't been able to stop himself taking a look behind the plastic cordon at the site of what used to be his building. Perched on top of the rubble was his lonely desk. He regarded the furniture, beyond rescue, of course.

With the unexpected fortune of time, he worked on the play. It seemed unlikely he would be able to use the college now, which was a pity. In which case he probably needed to call someone for help.

He jotted down tiny diagrams in an effort to imagine what the stage would look like, but essentially, he lacked the knowledge. Other people did this so maybe he could learn from them, he thought. So, he obtained the number of a local theatre company. Could he inspect the venue? Yes. They gave him the number for the stage manager.

"And would it be all right if I... Thank you. Thank you very much."

A thirty-minute journey. He studied the actors as they delivered their lines. The crew were recording it. It wasn't clear to him why. A rehearsal technique, potentially.

"We picked up the problem in the middle, and I think otherwise they met their marks," said the director (potentially). The inside of the local theatre was lined with vertical planks like the upturned hull of a wooden boat. It rose to an apex in the ceiling as though sinking, thought Eric.

He was sitting at home writing up his notes when Jim called him back.

"Hi, Jim."

"Eric. I'll cut to chase. The rumour is it was David Spurling."

"Right." Eric considered the news. "Was he targeting me?"

"I don't think so. There's no reason to think like that," said Jim. "We think it's simply because of where the college gave him a job. Could have been any department. But at least books don't explode like chemistry sets." *What about English teachers?* thought Eric. They could explode. The police were going to want to talk to him again. He had that strange feeling again of being caught up in something unstoppable, like an ocean wave. He stood at the back door, smoking. The question was why he'd done it. *If* David had done it. He'd spoken with David's parents after the earlier incident. They'd called him between classes and wanted to apologise on their son's behalf. Did the best they could to explain. They'd thanked him for not taking the matter further, which he'd never intended to. David was being punished, they had assured him – he put it to his lips. Now David was in a world of trouble.

13

That evening, as Eric took the kitchen waste out to the rubbish bins, a cyclist drifted over to the kerb beside him. It was Richard; Eric recognised him.

"Eleanor's not here tonight. She's at her mum's," explained Eric.

"I know," said Richard, setting his bike on the pavement. "I came to talk to you."

"Okay." This was certainly out of the blue. "Bring your bike." Richard followed him up the steps.

"Did you want a drink?"

"No thanks," said Richard.

"Okay." Eric encouraged him to sit down.

"So, what is it?"

"Umm, I… need to borrow some money." He looked at Eric and nodded.

"Okay," said Eric. "How much?"

"A thousand." Eric looked at him.

"I know it's a lot." Richard bit a fingernail.

"What's it for?"

"Umm," said Richard. "I can't tell you. I just have to fix something." To the limit of what he knew Eric understood that.

"It's quite suspicious."

"I know." Richard nodded calmly. Eric thought about it.

"You do realise the position this puts me in?"

"Yeah. But I wouldn't ask, you know, if it wasn't important. I can't ask Mum and Dad."

"Right. Assuming I give it to you, and you're not willing to tell me what it's for, can you at least assure me this will be the end of it?" Richard nodded. For the second time Eric led Richard up a flight of stairs.

"El said you're writing a play?"

"Yes," he said as he typed in the young man's bank details.

"Thanks, Eric," said Richard.

"Okay. Well, don't fuck it up. For both our sakes."

"I won't," Richard promised. Eric stood with one foot on the patio tiles and reflected on it.

'Don't forget your bike,' Eric had said, in an effort to be humorous. He accompanied Richard to the door. They shook hands and Eric watched as Richard cycled away. 'Stay in touch,' he said. Because he wanted to know when it was resolved.

He read for half an hour, mulling over one thousand pounds.

———•———

The next morning, he showered, ate breakfast, dressed, and got into the burgundy car. With the second interview he could see they were trying to profile David and understand the background.

"He had an outsider mentality. Is that right, do you think?"

"I wouldn't necessarily say so. He was struggling to come to terms with himself, as many young people are. But I wouldn't strictly say so, no." He had given Richard a thousand pounds…

"Most people who commit destructive crimes believe they're outsiders. Experts say it begins with a sense of exclusion and develops from there. Does that sound like David Spurling to you?"

"Er, no. I wouldn't say it was that dramatic. But I don't really know him."

"Uh huh. Are you aware of any precipitating triggers?"

"No," said Eric.

"And about the crash. Do you think the decisions made afterwards were considered by David to be an unfair punishment?"

"I didn't see or speak to David after the day we had at the hospital."

"Right. But the two of you had some kind of rapport, isn't that correct, Mr Crawford?"

"No, I don't think so," said Eric.

"Right. But would it still be fair to say that on the day we're talking about you became more than just strangers?"

"Well, obviously, if you put it in those terms. But, as I said, it was just that day."

"You said he was driving the vehicle directly at you?"

"Before he swerved, yes."

"And at the hospital he didn't want anyone contacting his parents?"

"That's right," nodded Eric.

"But you did."

"Yes. It seemed notifying his family was the right thing to do. He's not an adult."

"What sort of relationship did he have with his parents?"

"I think it was difficult. But it can be, can't it?"

"How do you know that?"

"His parents spoke to me after the incident, and they told me he was having a difficult time."

"At the college?"

"Generally, I think. You know I didn't actually teach David?"

They thanked him for his time, apologised for the inconvenience, smiled at him professionally. The officer, a DC Bradbury, then told him that he liked, if possible, to meet all the witnesses in a case. "Stir the soup," he said. Then he asked Eric how the college was dealing with the situation.

"Pragmatically," said Eric. "I'm actually moving into my new office today."

———•———

Eric and Miriam could hear the heavy machinery still working to clear the bricks and mortar, as they brushed shoulders in the stationery cupboard.

"Where did they put you?" he asked.

"Out of sight," she said. What Georgina had said, suddenly crossed his mind. Maybe now was the time to leave.

The afternoon he used to prepare for his resumption of teaching. He bought a leafy plant, which he put on the windowsill. Then at home, he put a potato in the oven to bake. The evening news released further information. That the college had given David the cleaning job and thus the access. He ate the potato.

The play resurfaced, as an odd sort of consequence, proving to be a stabilising force. And he paced the living room acting out the parts. The image he had of the boy's mother. Her head, as she lay in the hospital bed, covered by a net of sensors. The physician reading out to her Shakespearean quotations, like, "To be or not to be." Eric recited the famous lines. The electrical outputs scratching jaggedly across grided paper —

He met Georgina again that evening for a drink.

"Hi." He kissed her on the cheek. "How are you?"

"I'm all right," she said. "Alive at least." She looked at him. "It sounds like a fucking disaster on campus. I didn't know if I should call someone," she said.

"Yes. Thanks," he said, interrupted by hospitality. They sat down.

"What if you had worked late?"

"Well…" said Eric.

"Do you ever work late?" she smiled.

"Not as a rule. Not on campus," said Eric.

"You live quite close, don't you?"

"Yes."

"What was it? A month ago, we were here?" she said. "Seems like a long time." For what it was worth, 'Yes', she was still writing. "You got some time off?"

"Yes, a couple of weeks, but we're back now. They've moved me into the history department. It's cramped," said Eric.

"Did anyone think it might be me?" asked Georgina. (It was a joke, but Eric chose not to react for effect.) "You thought I might take my revenge by blowing you all up? Tell them I've got bigger fish to fry."

"I've been using the time to write my play," he told her.

"You know what this means, Eric?"

"What?" he said.

"It's just a matter of time before you're leaving," she smiled. "What's it about?"

"Well, it's about a boy who gets sent away to a school to learn how to write a story that will save the world."

"Where did that come from? David? I told you, didn't I, post-trauma-playwright-disorder. You're suffering from it too," she smiled and put the drink to her mouth.

"I hadn't thought about it like that, but I guess in part it must be inspired by David. You?" asked Eric.

"Well, you should know that you're playing with fire. You're sure you want the answer?" She squeezed the lime into her drink. "I'm going to get animated," she said, "and say lots of very righteous things, which I mean, actually. But, you know, that's all part of it. You've got to be brave. Take the risk of looking the fool," she said, lifting a finger. "But I can trust you, now I know you can't judge me." She smirked. "I want to write a play. Which, to me, means something simple. A problem on a basic level. So, for me, a challenge besets an ordinary family, for which the man *take note* assumes exclusive responsibility. It starts with the stage divided." Georgina used a beer mat to illustrate. "On the right the husband sits reading in the kitchen, his head against his hand." (She acts it.) "On the left of the stage, in an upstairs bedroom, a woman/his wife, stands silently folding linen. Ten seconds. Then she leaves the room to go to her husband, and our eyes follow her down the stairs into the kitchen. 'What is it?' she asks. 'A bill,' he replies. 'What for?' 'It's all right,' her husband says. 'But what's it for?' she asks. 'I said, don't worry.' And that's the premise and the play. A woman and her husband stuck in a trap."

"It sounds very concise."

"That's a good thing, is it?"

"Yes," Eric smiled.

"I hope so," said Georgina. "Where have you got to?" she asked.

"I've finished the second scene," said Eric.

Act 1, Scene 2: The Journey

Our hero, the boy, sits at the bus stop holding an ice cream in his hand.

"People ask me the strangest things," *he says (wrapping his tongue around the ice cream).* "Am I from the future? No. I'm not. But I tell them, that I was taught to write *the story* of the future." (*Lick.*) "I stand out, that's what they're getting at. They taught us that. That we would probably stand out. That's why you sent me away. They don't like me saying that, but it's true. We were taught this would happen. You'd think that not having a story would be obvious, but not everyone sees it that way or you've just gotten used to it, somehow, which seems impossible." (*Lick.*) "Other times it seems like impatience. If not now, when? Never? We're working on it right now, I tell them, and I give them the card. 'Check in on us,' I invite them. We're right there at the Office of Future Storytelling." (*Lick.*) "It's just on the coast road, before the pier, I have to say. If you really want to know. It's very important that we have trust and that's why we go out. The first thing they ask is where you came from. And I have to explain to be careful with memory. Memory can be dangerous. It casts a spell." (*He finishes the ice cream and drops the remains into the trash can.*) "But I'm not sure they understand that pleasure is such an irrepressible thing." (*We hear the sound of the sea against the shore.*) "I'll do my best to explain it to you. Here goes," *he says.*

"Perhaps I should have thought, but I didn't. It just seemed clear to me that my family were staying. We parked the car and I pushed down the button," *he says, thinking.* "The doctor who met my mother and I said, 'Let go of her,' and, 'Would I like to see the toys,' he said. I remember him because he had bruises or what were like bruises under his eyes. 'I'll see you in a moment,' she said. She smiled with a lot of emotion in her face. 'We'll look after her,' they told me. But they didn't take me to the toys, but instead into a small room, where they started to ask me questions.

"'It's very important that I ask you these questions.' The doctor took out the light and shone it in my eyes. Then he took my blood pressure and my temperature, you know, how they tie it around your arm. I could smell the stale coffee.

"'Okay, now we'd like you to watch this film.' He pulled out a computer and started typing. 'I want you to give it your complete attention,' and he turned the screen around. His face held a very serious and implacable expression. The image was a kaleidoscope of slow-spinning geometric shapes.

"'Watch it carefully,' he said. 'I'll be back in ten minutes.' And then, after ten minutes, 'Okay, that's enough.' He checked his watch. He re-examined me then. Held my wrist. 'Your heart rate is elevated. And your cortisol levels are increased. But apart from that you're a healthy boy,' he reported. 'Your mother is going to be very happy. Most children I see aren't so lucky.' I didn't understand a thing. Neither did I understand then, where we were going or then what it meant to be at a woman's bedside. She was my mother and she'd been overtaken by some sort of metamorphosis.

"'We're doing some tests, just like your tests.' They pulled plastic curtains around her bed. I could hear them reciting Shakespeare. 'It's to monitor your mother's brain, because it's become very overstimulated and we need to find out why.' The doctor put his hand on my back. 'I'll take you to the office,' he said. 'There's some more work for us.' We entered the office, and it contained more children my age. The doctor calmly opened a folder and turned it around.

I recognised my mother's handwriting. I read it, touching the paper. 'In the event that we are unable or unfit to care for our son...' I was to be evacuated. The doctor asked for my name and my address, which I recited, and he wrote down. 'It will be important for you, when you come back to us,' he smiled. And for the same reason, 'We need to take a blood sample to match you.' I sat still in the chair, while he uncapped and stuck in the needle. 'It's all right, don't be a baby,' he said. I knew, without any idea of how, that my life and the lives of the other children around me were about to change forever. I counted the blood-filled test tubes as he shook them and put them to one side. 'Wait there,' as he filled another phial. Waiting, I saw a blonde girl. She was skinny with long legs. She smiled, and I smiled back. 'This is your file,' he said. He put the pages into a new jacket, and then handed it to me. 'All right? You can join the others.' What queue? There was a snaking line of children. The blonde girl stood ignorant of me several bodies ahead. I had my answer. Someone took my hand. I was pulled down a flight of steps. The metal rang with the activity of my feet. I saw children getting on a bus. My hand was squeezed, and I was delivered to two men standing at the doors. Without hesitation, they waved me aboard. Through the window I looked up at the hospital. I saw more children's feet cascading down the steps. They were joining me on my trip. The engine started and the windows rattled. Our legs swayed at the knee, while our hands stayed fixed on our laps. A silence was created on that bus which, I think, only terrified children can manufacture. We got introduced to the twists and turns of the road. A boy with red hair was sitting next to me. We gathered up speed and distance. Roads got narrower and the scenery greener, as we left behind where we came from for wherever it was we were going. That rapid transition acquainted us with our first lesson. That a child can easily be made to forget. And that all remembering is really casting a spell.

"'Stand up now!' they shouted. 'I want you to go to the toilet. Go on!' Another man said, 'Here,' handing me a torch and a roll of toilet paper. I took them without a word and merged with the darkness. The grass around my feet was sodden. I picked out the other children at a hedgerow beside the edge of the field. There was the babbling of our urine.

"'Oi!' He grabbed me by the shoulder. 'If you're not going to use it, give it back. And get yourself on the fucking bus.' I handed him the roll of paper.

"'Come on now!' he said, at the other children. 'You've had your time!' The driver looked at me, but I was of no interest to him. I sat again at my seat and leant my body against the fabric. I began to wonder. I began to dream. Not of home, but of the shapes the doctor showed me.

"I woke up into daylight, and for an instant I had no memory. I saw that I was alone and that the faces of the other children stared at me. The same faces which, without uttering a word, relayed what had happened: that the boy previously sat next to me had gone. In my mind, suddenly, there was an image of him running through a field, with the sinews of the green crops grappling at his legs. In the distance, the beams of men with torches flew high. I don't know what made the red-haired boy run away.

"'What's your name?' they asked me when I arrived.

"'It's Ivor.' *(The squeak of the bus as it arrives. Our hero climbs on board to the tune of the engine. The pshht sound of the doors.)*

"I'm off to work. I'll see you in a bit," *he says, departing.*

END of Act 1, Scene 2

We observe Eric and the Storyteller sat across from one another in silence, the barrier between them dissolved. Then both men, with a symmetry of motion, lift water to their lips, drink and swallow contentedly.

"Dad?" interrupted Eleanor.

"Yes." He looked up calmly. Eleanor stood with her arms folded.

"I'm going to live with Mum."

"Why?" asked Eric, surprised. He looked at her with focused attention.

"You're not really here."

"Well, we should talk about it before you make a decision," said Eric, conscious that there would be ramifications.

"You're just working, Dad."

"Only at the moment." He closed the computer. "Just wait, please, before you make a decision."

"Okay," she sighed.

"It will be okay," Eric reassured her. "It's just there's a lot going on. But I'll try to be more present. I'm sorry," he said again. "It won't be forever." He got up and slipped his hands into his pockets. "I'll make us a nice dinner."

They sat together with their food and switched on the TV. He looked at his daughter and she looked at him.

"You know I'm still basically a child," said Eleanor. And then, "Who's Georgina?"

"We used to work together," said Eric.

14

Francesca had done all she could about the furore. She sat beside the fuselage window as the clouds passed silently underneath. Sofia, two seats, but a world away. She returned to the accusations being levelled at her. Now, it seemed, she had managed to betray everyone. Her art and her children. At sixty-two, the thought came to her: that perhaps she enjoyed being Monsieur Bickert, more than he did? She had done thirty years of business. That was right, of course. She massaged the ring on her finger. The plane pitched gently, spreading sunlight across her face.

"Would you like anything?" whispered the flight attendant.

"No. Thank you." Francesca shook her head. It had bought her the Regency house in London. She went on. It paid for the seats on this flight, she counted on her fingers, many thousands of feet above the ground. The book on Sofia's lap, and the driver who sat waiting to take them to London. Strange now to think about it. If the ice in her heart existed, then most likely it was because of Bertrand; or was that romantic? The car took them home, stopping first at Sofia's apartment. Francesca couldn't gauge if Sofia agreed with what she was doing. They had little to say to each other, except 'Goodnight'.

When the driver handed over her bags outside the house, Francesca thought, *Why not take him in?* He was a slim, attractive man in his mid-forties. The taboo made her want against the odds for those early years again. It was just nice to receive affection. She took off her clothes, showered and stood by the window. Everybody wished a thrill, even if you had to administer it yourself. She poured herself a drink. The small gated park inside the square contained period lamps. It had been what, three months, she thought, since she was last there? Did paying for it mean never enjoying it? After two dramatic years in Paris, she returned to England to live with her parents. A situation that descended into a nightmare. They simply did not exist in the same world any longer. Seemingly endless quarrels with her mother, territory fought over again and again. When her adopted country called her back, she grabbed the opportunity with both hands, but decided it was right to leave Eric behind. She never planned it. She switched hands, returning to her groin. Her thoughts after orgasm returned to the questions they were likely to ask. Why she was still involved in their case? What was in it for her? The press seemed adamant that they should simplify her activities. She scattered these thoughts in preparation across sheets of paper extracted from the bedside drawer. Adrian was picking her up at nine o'clock.

She had still seen Eric every year. Given him her best. Holidays and half-term trips to France. She had insisted that her parents leave him the house, not to her, so that he would be set up financially, which had worked out very well. A plan that had formed during one of those distant conversations conducted through teeth. She looked up and smiled. She had developed a habit by then, much to her mother's ire, of peppering her conversation with French phrases. When her mother realised that Eric could speak French better than English, it was the last straw. Her relationship with her father had been softer. He had loved her in a more forgiving way. She had thought genuinely that life would be more secure for Eric, and looking at it now, she thought again that she had been right. He had his own life, while Sofia remained in her shadow. All that travelling. This was the problem when they came home. She saw Sofia become listless, like a sailor on land.

'Why are you so angry with us?' her mother once snapped. Francesca didn't feign denial. Instead, she said, 'I don't know.'

'You were such a clever girl.'

'Meaning what, Mum?' Her mother had never understood why she hadn't told them she was pregnant. But that's precisely what she was weaning herself from. Her father didn't like it, but at least he got it. If she were brutally honest, she would say that she had needed Monsieur Bertrand Bickert.

15

"It was the same kid? Christ, you were the lucky one," said Joe. "Are you hearing this?"

"Yes," said Rebecca.

"He was trying to kill you?"

"No. I don't think so," said Eric.

"Presumably they'll try him, won't they?"

"Yes," said Eric.

"You'll be a witness?"

"Well, I wasn't there. But yes, probably."

"No," conceded Joe. "But where were you?"

"I bet we're the first with that joke," said Rebecca, resting the base of her glass on her arm. "Has it affected you?" she asked. "I'm certain it would me."

"I've had to think very carefully about what I said to David."

"I bet."

"What did you say?" said Joe.

"Well," smiled Eric, "I didn't say, 'Blow up my building'."

The three got up and took their bodies through to the dining table.

"Richard out?"

"Yes. We were the same at his age. I was always out," said Joe. "When did we last see him?" he asked Rebecca. "Sunday? He's probably covered in tattoos, got several girls pregnant. Developed a heroin habit."

Rebecca took the hot pan out of the oven and put it on the table.

"Smells great," said Joe.

"It does," agreed Eric.

"It's bean stew. Well," said Rebecca, "you can see that for yourself."

A ladle deposited its contents into their bowls.

"It's really good," said Eric.

"Thanks."

"It really is very good," added Joe.

"How did Eleanor react?" asked Rebecca.

"With shock, like me," said Eric.

"She's been staying with us," said Rebecca.

"She told me you kicked her out," said Joe.

"No, she didn't," said Rebecca. "This one needs some drama."

"It's my fault. I haven't been paying attention."

"Working?" asked Rebecca.

"I said, it must be that girl, because, let's face it, you're really quite lazy," smiled Joe.

"What girl?" asked Rebecca.

"Georgina," said Joe. "Eleanor told me all about it. Said you used to work together. Quite combustible, your office, isn't it, Eric?"

Before Rebecca could comment they were interrupted.

"Why aren't you asleep?" asked Rebecca. Alex shrugged.

"Is it because Eric's here? He won a prize at school, and he told me he wanted to tell you," she said. "Go on. Don't be shy now you've won the opportunity." The boy looked at his mother and then at the piece of paper in his hand.

"A man on a boat sails across the ocean. His boat starts to sink, so he lands on an island." The boy lifted up an illustration. "At one end of the island there is a volcano. At the other end is a mountain. In the daytime it's too hot and at night it's too cold. So, he sleeps on the volcano to keep warm and in the daytime, he goes to the mountain to stay cool."

Eric listened. "Your story sounds like an allegory." The boy looked at him.

"Don't be weird," said Joe. "You're weird enough already."

"You'll have to remember that word," said Rebecca. "You can remember it because it's got 'Lego' written in the middle. Al-lego-ry."

"Go on then. You've had your fifteen minutes," said Joe.

They waited until the boy had gone.

"It's sweet," said Rebecca. "But at the same time, I don't want to over-encourage him. And he get full of himself."

"Like Richard, you mean?" said Joe. Rebecca looked at her husband.

"Come on," he said. "We spoiled him."

"I think it's time to smoke. Don't you?" She looked at Eric.

"Why didn't you tell me that you were seeing someone?" asked Rebecca as they stood outside.

"I'm not. Eleanor's just stirring."

"Oh… Do you like her? You can, you know."

"Yes, I know."

"What is it you're working on?" asked Rebecca. "You haven't gone off the rails, have you?"

"It's a school play."

———•———

He thanked Joe and Rebecca for looking out for Eleanor. Joe said, adopting the habit he commonly had of saying something controversial, 'They're eighteen and the leeches are not our responsibility'. Eric decided to walk. He felt as light as air. At home, he opened the taps to fill the bath. When the bath was full, he sat down. The heat rose up in listless curls. What the Storyteller had kept from Eric was the curious effect of their shared perspective. The ordinary world got on with business, while they were stranded.

———•———

At his desk, the Storyteller sat preoccupied with the annual speech he had to give. He gave it every year, on the same day, and at the same time in Laureate Square. This was where the story of the city was told. Always a big crowd, always a sense of occasion. The people in the city looked forward to it. Their story for the year. And if the story wasn't good enough, they held it against him. In that sense the story determined his year too. A good year followed a good story. This year, of course, was especially important. It was his last chance to impress upon people what he wanted to say. It was different this year also because of the letters. The letter from Anna which brought him to Eric. In the end the beginning. At Laureate Square, past the network of redbrick streets, past Caleb Street. He tapped the desk pensively with his fingers. The date for it was marked in his diary. More important than the pages of his books.

―――•―――

While we admire the Storyteller, Eric lies on the other half of the stage blanching in the tub. His attention focuses no further than his toes. He reaches out for the cigarette, puts it to his lips, looking out, but not seeing. A moment passes and then the Storyteller rolls in a fresh sheet of paper. Eric promptly stands, cigarette between his lips, placing his dripping body on the mat.

The table, which now features a picture of Alex' imaginary island, has become a repository of peculiar memorabilia. Eric reappears downstairs by the back door. The night air is mild. The garden a greyed-out spectacle, squared off by brick walls. The garden isn't something Eric takes much interest in, yet curiously he appreciates it tonight. He turns to locate the moon. The mottled darker areas on the surface are like patches of lichen.

―――•―――

"You must be wondering, why they sent away a child. The difference between you and me," *the boy said*, "is obvious. I have a future. You don't. A child is closer to reality. The rate of decay makes it true, a fact no adult wants to accept. We call it the *'Critical Window'*. The period during which a child learns how to see the world. That's why children are so important..." Eric perched his elbow. He would call this child Ivor, because the name Ivor had the remoteness he was looking for. Eric left the paragraph unfinished.

Tomorrow he would hear from Latham. 'Sit down.

How is everything – it's certainly been a year.' Which was a dramatic understatement. For the moment, Eric was content to remain in the present, contemplating Ivor.

———•———

"The way the college sees the present situation is as an opportunity," Latham explained. "Natural that we should consider the English programme. I know that's difficult, but I'm sure you can see. And it means – I won't beat around the bush – personnel, Eric." Eric looked up at the ceiling.

"Don't worry, I'm not trying to frighten you," Latham smiled. "You've been with us a long time."

"Yes," said Eric. Seeing the image of a sell-by date.

"And I know in that time, you've specialised the curriculum."

"We play to our strengths, I think," said Eric.

"That's the point, really. I need to bring us into line with what other colleges are offering. Whether we like it or not. And I was hoping to enlist your help. Before you react," Latham lifted his hand, "let me just say I recognise with an independently minded faculty that it won't be easy. But I can assure you it's necessary."

"What do you want us to teach?" asked Eric.

"Well," Latham considered the question, "that's for another day. We're not trying to rush this through."

"Right," said Eric.

"That aside, it's clear from your student feedback" – Latham selected a sheet of paper – "that our students regard you as a very stimulating teacher. We, of course, need to be sure that it equates to results. I'm not telling you there's a problem, Eric, I'm just being honest with you. And look, whatever happens, I'll make sure you have some time off. The college knows you're acting on its behalf in this unfortunate matter with David Spurling. I'm aware also that you've taken up the challenge to enter the competition. So, I can see that you're working hard for us. In that spirit I'm more than happy to grant you use of the drama department."

"Thank you," said Eric.

———•———

Eric got out of bed that morning and showered.

———•———

On the path outside Latham's office, he was met by Tina.

"Hello," she said.

"Hello," said Eric.

"Have you been fired?" Eric looked at her. She smiled.

"No. Why?" he asked.

"I saw you coming out of the dean's office. And we had to fill in our evaluation forms."

"Oh. What did you say?"

"I said, you were doing okay."

"Thanks," said Eric.

"If you'd given me an A."

"I gave you a B+." Eric put the filter to his lips and began searching for his papers. "Is there something I can help you with?" he said.

"I'm on my way to your class."

"Right. Then I'd better give you these then," and he gave Tina the keys. "Tell the others I'll be five minutes."

The class was squeezed into his new digs in the history department.

"I'm sorry," he said. "About the space. Umm. Okay. Perhaps as it's a short piece, Sam, you could read it for us?"

"Okay," said Sam, obediently.

The story they were reading was one Eric tended to reserve for the right students. It was about a musician who blocked his ears with wax.

"Pyotr Pishka sat practising scales on his violin, while his wife Mischa sat reading downstairs. As his fingers travelled in a blaze up and down the neck of the instrument, his mind travelled back to a day at school, when, let out on account of everyone but him succumbing to dysentery, he explored the city for the very first time. Those around him adjudged snobbishly that he had been spared the bug on account of his humble origins. The country was strictly segregated and even illness was expected to follow suit. With no students, or teachers to teach, the regimental lectures were abandoned. 'So,' his kind master, Pavel, said, 'go out, my boy, and see the city.' Twelve years old, held as a charge of the school from the age of seven, Pyotr Pishka had never been outside the school gates unaccompanied before. Without needing to be offered the gift twice, he set out clutching the iron key Pavel had given him. The immediate impression of so many people was dazzling. Where were they going? Pyotr dove eagerly into the world. (Not to forget that this was the first chance the world had to glimpse Pyotr.) The school, of course, made Pyotr dress like a gentleman, which meant he proved immensely courteous to the people he met. Prompting them to be kind to him. 'Not to mind you, young sir,' 'Go on, try a piece of this,' 'Take a slice of that,' 'It's our pleasure, we assure you.' By noon his stomach was more than full. So he took refuge in the park. At first alone, he sat monitoring the sway of the trees. Then, after a few minutes, he was joined by a well-dressed man who sat down on the bench next to him. Whom Pyotr watched as he unpacked an exquisite-looking lunch.

"'What is that?' asked Pyotr, pointing. The man looked round.

"'A cat,' the man said. 'You do not recognise a cat? Surely,' he said with surprise, 'at your age you should recognise a cat?'

"'I play the violin,' said Pyotr.

"'I see. Are there no cats in music?' the man asked.

"'None,' said Pyotr.

"'Then you should correct this mistake,' the man said, with a smile, 'and write a symphony about cats!' Amused by the boy's innocence, the jowls on the man's face rose up, forming the shape of two rosy apples.

"'I shall,' said Pyotr.

"'Good boy,' he commended. 'And I shall be the first to hear it.' The man then paused. 'What's your name?'

"'It's Pyotr Pishka,' said Pyotr. When Pyotr returned the other students showed no interest in his adventure. Some of the boys laughed and asked him whether, instead of the belly, it had got him in the head. It was 'rube disease', they cackled. They had devised, over time, several ways of teasing him.

"Remembering it, Pyotr wondered if it was 'rube disease' that prevented him from enjoying his performances. These past weeks he had been wracking his brains without success. He needed, he decided, to visit his friend, Tanic. By that hour, he checked the clock on the wall above him, Tanic would be sitting in the tavern on Bruegel Street. He knew Tanic went there after the hours he spent in his workshop. Like Pyotr, he was born in a local village, and it was this that underpinned their friendship. While Pyotr had studied music, Tanic had learned the practical crafts of boat making, house building, the mending of threshers and cotton looms. He knew everything that Pyotr did not (or most at least), so if anyone was going to help him to see things differently, it was Tanic. Pyotr put on his heavy coat and told Mischa that he was going to the tavern on Bruegel Street. In response she simply lifted her face and smiled.

He found Tanic just as he suspected, sitting in the wooden nook by the fire. He bought them each a pint of ale and then set about describing to Tanic his pains.

'"Pyotr,' remarked Tanic, 'you are ambergris. Do you know this?' Pyotr shook his head.

'"What is ambergris?' he asked.

'"It comes from whales. And it's very rare. It's made in their bellies and they use it to protect themselves from sharp objects. They vomit it into the ocean,' said Tanic, 'and then it floats around until it gets washed up. Or we catch the whale.' He paused.

'"Why am I ambergris?' asked Pyotr with deep interest.

'"Because,' said Tanic, 'of what people do with ambergris.'

'"What do they do?'

'"Fix perfume, of course,' said Tanic, with a broad smile. But Pyotr didn't understand.

'"They fix perfume,' repeated Tanic. 'The whale doesn't know that what it vomits is useful. And would probably find the idea disgusting that we should put it on our skin. The whale doesn't know he's producing ambergris. Doesn't know how rare it is or that people prize it and are willing to pay large sums for it. What it does for us, like you, Pyotr, with your violin, is something the whale can't share in or understand. Vomit to some is gold to others,' he smiled. 'And what do you suppose would happen if the whale knew it produced ambergris?'

'"I don't know,' said Pyotr. 'Be very rich?'

'"Do you suppose the whale would stop making it?'

"'No,' said Pyotr. 'Because it protects it.'

"'Exactly,' said Tanic. 'That is the point exactly. That you don't share or appear to reap the joys of what you sow does not change your nature. Doing so would almost certainly be to your disadvantage, like the whale. But,' said Tanic, adopting a thoughtful expression, 'being prepared to ask yourself the question means you are brave like the whale.' Pyotr ordered himself another drink. He sat opposite Tanic and thought. He was very lucky, he told himself, to have a friend like Tanic, who didn't try to swindle him. He departed the tavern and staggered home, where he settled upright by the fireplace. After several hours of snoring, and with sunlight piercing the curtains, he awoke. He told Mischa at breakfast about whales and ambergris.

"The following week, beside the conductor, Golubev, for the season's gala performance, Pyotr sat nervously with his ears now unplugged. He wanted to see if he could tolerate the music. The stakes for him were high. As it turned out his catastrophic thoughts were given little air to breathe (*did Golubev know?* Pyotr wondered) as from the corner of his eye the white baton began thrusting and bobbing; the blare from the trumpets, the strings swelled, escorting Pyotr, as if he were carried by a flood, to the point where he had to put the violin to his chin. The first note left his hands, the horsehair sliding over gut. He swayed his torso, his arms and elbows, and moved his fingers. As he played, he heard nothing. Not a note of music. Vibrations there were, but no symphony. What else could he do but keep playing? Despair threatened to envelop him, but something else, just as suddenly, took hold, as a result of which a smile. It didn't matter that it had stopped working in him if it galvanised other people. When, afterwards, members of the audience came to see Pyotr, it was to tell him, 'They had never heard anything like it.' He thought of Tanic's advice, there was nothing else for him to do, but to play.

"Toward the end of his time at music school the man he'd met that day in the park came to the school to see him. At first this was as an unrecognisable figure at the back of his graduation recital. By now he had written the piece about cats. The recital being an opportunity to draw a crowd and hopefully attract employment with an orchestra. At the very end of the evening the man sought him out. 'Pyotr Pishka?' He heard his name. At the man's instruction they went for a walk. He told Pyotr, after that day in the park, that he had spoken to his master, Pavel. There was nothing for him to worry about, he assured Pyotr, offering to promote the young violinist with all the means at his disposal. That night, at the gala performance, Phillipe sat at the back clapping his hands, calling out, 'Bravo!' He then collected his top hat and cane and departed for the night. As his smart shoes landed, one after the other, on the paving stones, he recalled that what he had seen in Pyotr was not a musical gift, but a strangeness in character that meant the boy was bound to do something. This recollection of their conversation brought a smile to his face."

"Okay, so what do you think?" Eric asked his students.

"Well, he's an idiot," said Tina. "A savant figure."

"That can be a cause of suffering, can't it?" said Eric. "You don't think Pyotr learns anything? You think that's all a red herring?"

"A red whale," said Javid.

"Sam, you normally have something interesting to say?" said Eric.

"I just think, what if Pyotr is right? And night after night it is an empty performance. His friend doesn't judge what's right or wrong; he naturalises everything. Pyotr is like the whale. And does what he does. So, actually, I think the violinist is the clever one."

"Maybe it's Mischa," said Eric, with a smile.

Eric went home, after class. He put on some music to goad Pyotr Pishka. He made some casual notes of what his class had said. Then he relaxed with dinner.

———•———

Peace didn't last. We see him steer the burgundy car home from Madeline's. Because it was midnight, his tyres caroused over the damp tarmac.

'What had happened?' They'd stabbed a boy, or someone had. Richard got home with blood on him. It was his friend Vincent's blood. This had summoned Eric to Madeline's house.

Her living room that evening served as a courtroom. He turned left into Clermont Road. Got out. He now felt quite awake. The mystery pilot in charge of the world had altered course. That's how he found himself driving back from Madeline's in the early hours. Eleanor sat in front of them, unrecognisable to him. Let's have some of the facts. Eric tried to remember. She went to a house party that a boy called Vincent had organised. Those friends included Richard and Darrell. It was a sort of farewell party, before some of them went off to university. Eleanor had gone with her friend, Pedra. They'd put their drinks in the fridge. It was nothing Eric or Madeline hadn't done. There were drugs at this party. When Richard got home, Rebecca went crazy.

'It's all right, Mum, it's not mine,' he'd told her. There had been a phone call from one of the other parents.

'It was nothing to do with him,' said Eleanor defensively, meaning Richard. 'It was a group of boys. And it happened in front of the house. Somehow a knife had found its way from the kitchen.'

'Yes, we know,' said Eleanor. Fiddling before them with the hem of her dress.

They rang the police.

'The boy?'

Vincent.

'Is he going to be all right?'

'We don't know.'

A thousand pounds.

The spinning bulbs of the ambulance.

They had attacked the vehicle while the boy lay bleeding.

The moon was exceedingly bright.

Eric undressed.

He drew the curtains.

The kids were all right.

16

Rebecca sat beside the bookshelves in the back room, with steam gently rising from a cup of coffee. Light from the window on her face. And the sound, in the kitchen, of the washing machine spinning Richard's clothes.

"All right?" She looked up at Richard.

"Yeah." He zipped up his bag.

"Take it seriously."

"I will," he said.

"Have you got money?" she asked.

"Yes."

"And don't be rude to him."

"I won't." He stopped and looked at her. He was several inches taller than her. Then he made a joke.

"Don't be ridiculous," she said. "And be careful on your bike." Richard walked the bicycle from the shelter into the road, put his leg over the saddle, spun the pedal and put his foot down.

Rebecca took up the mug. "Boyfriend," she repeated, prompting the haze of cigarette smoke. Rebecca Lark. She found herself touching her lips. She wondered about this boy, Vincent. If he was going to be all right. The impact this might have on their lives. Events dating back to sperm and the egg. Rebecca Lark. A regular middle-class childhood in her case, an older sister, Joan, a good school, stable enough parents. Her first boyfriend, Geoff Carr. The second, Dominic Priest, a vet now, she'd heard, and then, Joe. By which point you'd found out how it was going to go. She put the mug to her lips. She had a strong sense that their household was a collection of individuals, try as she might, passing in a hall of mirrors. She then heard Joe's feet on the stairs. And watched him as he appeared in the kitchen.

"Did you get much sleep?" he asked, filling up the kettle.

"No," she said. They defaulted to the sound of Richard's clothes.

"Is there anything you want me to do?" he said.

"No," said Rebecca, sipping coffee.

"Is there something wrong?" he asked her, emptying boiling water into the mug.

"What do you mean?"

"You tell me. A day doesn't go by when it's not something with these kids." He took milk out of the fridge and poured some into his tea. "I'll leave, if you want me to?" He took a bowl off the shelf and then filled it with cereal.

"Don't be ridiculous," she said.

———•———

"This is it?" asked Richard, as he stepped into Eric's office. He looked left, then right.

"Yes," said Eric. "It is now."

Richard acknowledged it with a nod. He unzipped his bag

and took out an envelope.

"I brought this." He put it on Eric's desk.

"Okay, thanks." The elastic band wrapped around it formed a shape that needed no explanation.

"I'm not going to university." Richard sat down. "I don't want to study."

"Okay," said Eric. What defined Richard's face, which Eric regarded, was a wide brow, more exaggerated than his father's. The skin as white as snow. Richard had this born with innate knowledge thing. It was the reason Eleanor liked him, and it was a good reason to like Richard. It was the reason he liked Richard. It seemed so strange that Joe and Rebecca couldn't see it.

"Your friend. Is he all right?"

"I think so." Richard shrugged. "He wasn't really my friend."

"I gathered," nodded Eric.

"Wish you could tell Mum."

"It's nice to be thought of as someone to turn to, isn't it?" said Eric.

"I suppose so. Mum expects you to convince me, doesn't she?" said Richard.

"Yes. I think so. I think she wants what she thinks is best for you."

"Best for her."

Eric watched him. "I imagine she doesn't want you wasting your time," he said.

"Parents have the wrong idea about their kids." Richard sat back in the chair.

"Why don't you tell them what you're telling me? Seems like you've thought about it," suggested Eric.

"Yeah," said Richard, but without sounding committed to the idea.

"It's really the only option I can see. Or I can talk to her if you want?" said Eric.

"No." The eyebrows formed a trench. "That won't work. Then she'll think I'm a coward."

"Parents want their kids to have good friends," said Eric. "They recognise that's important."

"Yeah." Richard bit the inside of his lip casually.

"Show them you've thought about it," said Eric, "that's my advice. From what I know, you're smart enough. I'd say the same to Eleanor."

"Yeah, but you're different," said Richard.

"I'm not sure I am," said Eric. "I want the same for Eleanor that Rebecca wants for you. I wouldn't be too proud to ask for our advice. That's my advice."

At Eric's door, Tina knocked a hand, and, not receiving an answer, turned the handle.

"Oh sorry," she said, and then, "Hi, Richard."

"Hi," he said back.

"I had an appointment with you," she told Eric. "To discuss the assignment." Her eyes fell on the envelope of money. "Or I can come back?"

"Just a few minutes," said Eric.

"Okay." Tina nodded.

"So, I think that's all I can tell you," said Eric, putting the money in his drawer. Richard nodded.

"Thanks. Can you tell Mum I was polite?"

"Yes," smiled Eric. Richard left the room and Tina entered. They went through the questions she had. And then Eric stayed behind to work.

Act 1, Scene 3: The School

"At the school, where they sent us, we were woken up every morning by the sound of the church bell," *said Ivor,* "we should be in the chapel."

The day started with a video sermon. Even for Ivor, memory was a dangerous thing. It brought forth ghosts from his student days.

"Who's he talking to?" *said Deborah*

"Is he casting a spell?" *said Suzanne, which for them meant indulging nostalgia.*

"Our favourite sermons are *The Category Plays*," *said Deborah.*

"I like the painter with his white beard," *said Suzanne.*

"I feel sorry for the boy with the target on his chest," *said Charlie.*

"I like Mr Y," *said Ivor, joining his friends.*

"Everyone likes Mr Y," *said Deborah. Which was absolutely true.* "Did you hear?" *she said.*

"What?" *they said.*

"That they're sending one of us home." *The student they were sending home was Ivor, of course.*

"How do you know that?" *said Suzanne.*

"It's just a rumour, I think," *said Charlie.*

"They've got to send one of us, eventually," *said Deborah. They all agreed but didn't say so or do anything to suggest they did.* "Shall we show them the sermons now?"

The sermons took on the stayed narratives of God, Love and Beauty. If the students were ever to tell new stories, they would have to be inoculated against the old. The idea, for Eric, of showing these video sermons in a chapel was obvious; the church was the only physical space for contrary ideas that he knew. The students had to watch them before the critical window closed and their minds got overtaken by habit. And he thought there was something comical, anyway, about the purpose of students' isolation being to watch TV.

"Come on!" *said Deborah.*

I

An old man comes on with the aid of a stick and sits down. A long and dirty beard, thick bushy eyebrows, a bald head and the protrusion of a misshapen nose, sitting in a gallery. The old man's eyes are obscured beneath his brow and appearing through his shabby clothes a frail body. He sits there, a moment, shoulders rounded, a body swathed in a painter's smock. When he does speak his voice is soft.

"I wonder," *he says*, "now. If I should have had a family, a wife and a child?" *He speaks slowly.* "At least a girl. But I couldn't," *he whispers. A female visitor passes in front of him.* "Easy to think about. Hard to do," *he chuckles. He coughs and then with a deep breath clears his throat.* "I'm a painter. Painted all my life. Made up for what I felt was missing by making pictures. Followed what was inside." *He points at his temples.* "But I tell you," *he laughs,* "there are no mysteries, not like I thought there were. It's the outside world that counts. Took me a long time to realise that." *Another person passes in front of him.* "Everything is outside," *he repeats. With both fingers he points at the audience.* "It's people and the world I should have been worrying about." *He pulls away the beard and opens his robe, straightens his back and stretches his legs.* "By the middle years I'd made a life out of it. But time catches up with you, and by then, you know…" *He puts his hands down either side of him and crosses his legs.* "You're made that way. I took normal jobs when I had to. A pension," *he smiles.* "I could certainly use that. And what about her? Go for it. But I was a sucker and had been from the beginning." *The painter takes off his mask, removes his robe, leaving them beside him. A young man again. He points his two fingers at his temples, and then at the audience.* "The mysteries," *he says. Laughing, he stands up.*

II

"Oh, I love you," *said the first character.* "Do you love me?" *He came dressed as a soldier and is armed with a gun.*

"Yes. I love you," *she said.* "Tell me what it means?"

"My love, you make me feel special," *he said. The rest of the cast laugh. The soldier looks at them for a moment but then continues.*

"It makes me feel that the universe and all of time is telling me that it is right for me to exist at this place and at this time. Love makes me believe it." *A second time they laugh.*

"Why are they laughing?" *she asks.*

"Because they are not in love." *The cast then begin to chant,* "Test it! Test it!"

"What would you have me do?" *the soldier says. He looks down for a moment and then, without explaining himself, takes out the gun.*

"If love be a true force." *A loud bang. The cast gasp.*

III

"When I was twelve, I got mugged by some boys. They took my money. I thought it didn't matter because I was a good person. They were bad people and so they would be punished. When I told the Reverend Keith about it, he replied that because of the way I reacted, I could be a priest one day.

"'Just follow the goodness inside!' the reverend said and blessed me. 'The goodness inside is the will of the Lord.'

"When I left school, I got a job at our local supermarket. It was boring. I wanted to do something I could really enjoy, but I had the Lord telling me that the supermarket was the right time and place for me to exist, and I didn't want to question that feeling. Everything was all right when I thought about things like that. It didn't even matter when I got into trouble. I was caught with Tom, playing with the trolleys in the car park. We tried to collect as many as we could in a snake, and I hit someone's car. I had asked Tom before whether he believed in God. Tom said he did, meaning that both of us were at the supermarket because God wanted us to be there, and we both had the goodness inside, which was the work of the Lord."

Tom steps forward. The shirt he's wearing is circled with blood.

"'Are you happy living with your mum and dad? Only I'm thinking of moving out,' he said. 'We wouldn't have to spend a penny on food.' So, I agreed to move in with Tom.

"'That's great. I'll start looking,' he said. It was easy on the money side of things, because we earned the same pay. So, I let Tom decide. He found this two-bedroom flat. Mum and Dad helped me move in, even though the goodness inside didn't want them to. On the second weekend we had a party. We invited all our friends, and everyone had a good time. The next day, Tom was busy puking, so I did the cleaning. But I didn't mind because I'd had such a good time at the party. When it came to our first month's rent Tom surprised me when he said he couldn't pay. 'What do you mean?' I asked. 'I've spent it,' he said. 'On what?' 'I do something,' he said, without elaboration. 'I'm sorry. I normally have a profit. But not this time.' 'But I won't have anything left,' I told him. He just shrugged. So, I paid that month's rent for both of us. And because there was nothing left, we ate all of our meals in the supermarket. The next time we had a party some of Tom's other friends came. Most of the time they were busy teasing him. I learned that it had something to do with money. But I kept out of it, at first. Until something inside me told me I had to protect myself. That was when I picked up a knife. Tom was telling them he'd sort it out, but they weren't interested. When they saw the knife, it became a fight. I felt like I had to protect myself. I know I cut one of them. The boy lay on the carpet with a look of horror on his face. When I blinked, I saw Tom. Our friends by then were screaming. One of them called the police. I didn't say or do anything. When the police arrived, they handcuffed me. I was still holding the knife. I didn't want to let it go. It was still making me feel safe. I believed the Lord had made me good inside. The universe and all of time was telling me it was right for me to exist at this place and at this time, and I didn't want to question that feeling. Everything felt all right when I thought about things like that. When I went to court the judge said I had poor judgement and sent me to prison. That's where I am, trying to figure out how I got here." *The young man sits there and doesn't move. He just gets older. (An effect achieved by a light projection.)*

With the last sermon, Eric had something very special in mind. He tipped water into the tray beneath the plant on the windowsill, while he waited for the printer to finish printing. He settled the pages. The fourth and final instalment.

Mr Y

A shop clerk, his legs crossed reading a newspaper. The paper is so large it conceals him entirely, except for his fingers. He closes the newspaper to turn the page and then, without taking any notice of the audience, reopens it. The shop sells a variety of board games represented by coloured boxes stacked on a table. One stack red, one green and the last yellow. The clerk raises his dramatically over-sized newspaper. On the back of it is printed in bold type the word, 'Transformation'. From the interior the shop façade appears back to front, but it is easily read as 'Brain's Games'. The bell to the shop then jerks. It is a simple bell tied to a piece of string. Mr Brain closes his newspaper, stands and strides towards the door. There in the middle of the stage he greets his customer.

"Good day!" *Mr Brain exclaims, breezily, opening his arms. Mr Brain projects a broad smile.*

"Hello," *says Mr Y,* "I'm looking for—"

"Meaning?" *interrupts Mr Brain.*

"Pardon me?"

"You're here for 'meaning' sir? The big M," *repeats Mr Brain, his smile only partially diminished.*

"Well, I suppose you could put it that way."

"It is best to get it out in the open," *says Mr Brain.* "Tell it like it is."

"Yes," *says Mr Y nervously.*

"So, what sort of meaning were you thinking of?" *the shop clerk enquires.*

"What have you got?" *asks Mr Y. Mr Brain turns to look at the audience in disgust at the customer's ignorance.*

"There are three basic types," *says Mr Brain.* "Did you know that?"

"No," *says the customer.*

"It's not necessary," *says Mr Brain.* "Some people do, some people don't. It all works out the same in the end."

"Okay," *says Mr Y. The shop clerk lures him to the table.*

"As I said, there are three basic types. But we can have each one of them adjusted to suit your particular needs. We have 'Love'," *Mr Brain points to the red box,* "perhaps the most obvious. Then there's 'God', which is traditional, but not so popular. Trends come and go. And finally, the strangest perhaps, 'Art'. Each one in its own way a perfectly good form of meaning guaranteed to produce the appropriate experience for the individual of validation, uniqueness and so forth. It is just a matter of preference, which one suits you best. I'm sure you have some idea of which way you lean, sir. Nearly everybody does." *The customer clutches his chin and gazes at the shop clerk.*

"Can I think about it for a moment?"

"Yes, of course, sir. You would be wise to do so. It is a very big decision. If you need anything just ask." *The shop clerk smiles obsequiously and backs away, before finally retreating altogether to the newspaper at his desk.*

Mr Y picks up one of the red boxes. He weighs it in his hands and then shakes it. On the back of the box is written its title in the same bold type as the print on Mr Brain's newspaper. Mr Y then returns the box, fitting it neatly.

Mr Brain lowers his paper to look at the audience. "Everyone comes to my shop," *he says, smiling.* "And they always go home with something. It makes me so pleased. I really can't tell you how pleased." *The bell trills again.* "Excuse me," *he tells the audience, getting to his feet.*

"Hello." *The new customer glances at the audience.*

"Welcome back, sir!" *exclaims the shop clerk. The two men shake hands.*

"How are you?" *asks the shop clerk earnestly.*

"Well," *says the new customer lugubriously. He wears a white smock which is daubed with colour and is holding a palette.* "If I'm honest I'm lacking in inspiration. I've come straight from my studio."

"I'm terribly sorry to hear that, sir," *says Mr Brain.* "One moment." *The Artist remains standing forlorn and immobile at the centre of the stage while Mr Brain hurries forwards to the games table and snaps up a yellow box, placing it in The Artist's free hand.*

"Oh, thank you! I'm so grateful," *replies The Artist.*

"Don't worry! It is my pleasure," *says Mr Brain.*

"I…" *begins The Artist. But the clerk reads his expression.*

"There's plenty in your account to cover it, sir."

"Oh good," *says The Artist.* "There's never too high a price to pay for peace of mind." *The Artist and Mr Brain laugh together. The Artist's eyes then move to observe Mr Y standing beside the table.*

"Who's this chap?" *whispers The Artist. Mr Y is holding onto the same yellow-coloured box. While Mr Brain and The Artist had been talking, he had been examining it, weighing it and shaking it.*

"A new customer…"

"I see," *says The Artist.* "Is he… an Artist too? He has a yellow box."

"The customer hasn't made a choice," *answers Mr Brain.*

"Oh!" *exclaims The Artist, smiling.* "Because I don't need any competition." *The Artist then returns his attention to Mr Brain.*

"Thank you, Mr Brain. I am very grateful." *They then begin to say their goodbyes.*

"Just take a seat while I write you up a ticket," *says Mr Brain. There are three chairs to the left of the clerk's table.*

"Yes, of course." *The Artist prepares to sit down. As Mr*

Brain returns to his desk the shop bell rings for a third time, catching his attention.

"Good day, madam!" *exclaims Mr Brain. The shop clerk dutifully approaches The Young Woman.*

"Hello," s*he says brightly. The Young Woman is carrying a greetings card with the image of a heart on the cover. Mr Brain points towards the card.* "I don't need to ask, do I?" *he says.*

"No, you don't." *She is gleeful and smiles back at him.*

"So, how are you?" *asks Mr Brain.* "I think it was only last week that I saw you."

"That's right, Mr Brain! My, you've got a good memory!"

"It certainly helps."

"I'm very well, thank you," *she says.*

Mr Brain goes to the games table to retrieve for her a red-coloured box. Mr Y is now holding the same colour in his hands, carefully scrutinising the print on the reverse. He hasn't paid The Young Woman any attention. Mr Brain looks at Mr Y and then casts his eyes to the audience.

The Young Woman snatches the box from Mr Brain and clutches it to her chest. "Thank you," *she says. She then takes an interest in Mr Y standing in line with her downstage.*

"Is he in love too?" *she asks, assuming she is correct.*

"I'm sorry, madam, I can't tell you," *the clerk replies.* "The customer has not made a choice."

"Oh…" *says The Young Woman, confused.* "How can he not know?"

"Some people aren't as lucky as you are. Speaking of which, how is your young man?"

"Well —" *she begins.*

"Am I right in thinking he is a soldier?" *interrupts Mr Brain.*

"Yes! Do you remember everything, Mr Brain? He's on duty, so I won't see him again for three weeks. Do you remember, Mr Brain, when both of us were here together and you made us cups of lovely tea? He is so handsome."

"Would you like to take a seat?" *says Mr Brain.* "While I get you a ticket?"

"Yes," *she says.* "I can see you're very busy." *The Young Woman promptly sits down beside The Artist, who is holding on to his yellow box. They eye one another agreeably.*

"You look very beautiful," *says The Artist.*

"Thank you," *she says.*

Mr Brain hastily scribbles on a piece of paper and hands it to The Artist. He tells him that, "All of the terms and conditions remain the same."

"Thank you so very much," *responds The Artist. Finally, a Young Man arrives and bursts into the shop. There is no time for Mr Brain to be alerted by the sound of the bell. The Young Man heads straight for the table and takes a green box. He is in such a hurry that he knocks one of them to the floor.*

"Can I pay for this!" *asks The Young Man.*

"I'm just dealing with another customer," *replies Mr Brain.*

"Please," *says The Young Man.* "I've got to go to a party."

"Surely you can wait a minute or two?" *says Mr Brain.*

"Yeah. Okay." *While Mr Brain is writing The Young Woman's ticket, The Young Man looks over at the two people sitting on the chairs.* "You're an Artist," *he says, nodding vigorously, rocking his feet.* "I love Art. Makes you feel good inside. And Love too," *he says, looking at The Young Woman.*

"What party are you going to?" *she asks.*

"Just a party," *The Young Man says.* "At my flat. I've got to let them in."

At the front of the stage Mr Y picks up the green box spilt on the floor. He then returns it neatly to the remaining boxes.

"Thanks, mate," *says The Young Man. Mr Y raises his hand and begins to walk towards the door.*

"Excuse me!" *calls out Mr Brain.* "Is something wrong?"

"No," *says Mr Y, who turns back to face him.* "I've decided not to choose today," *he says. The Young Woman and The Artist stand up from their seats.*

"But," *says Mr Brain, horrified,* "everyone who comes to my shop makes a choice." *The three other customers each nod, uttering,* "Yes."

"Well," *says Mr Y, glancing at them, before returning his attention to Mr Brain.* "I can't make this decision." *There is a pause, and no one says anything. Mr Y leaves through the shop door. The bell trills hollow.*

END of Act 1, Scene 3

17

Eric paced the floor with the play in one hand, and a sandwich in the other. Georgina was already at the stage of rehearsals, which were taking place at a community hall she'd found. He turned his head to the clock, the half-eaten sandwich carried further into the living room. That was when his feet came to a stop. He remembered that Saturday meant Eleanor. He'd fucked the weekend.

"Hi, Dad." She closed the house door.

"Hi." She saw him standing there.

"You forgot, didn't you?" she said, the accusation landing firm and square on his shoulders.

"No," said Eric feebly.

"Right." She passed him into the kitchen, where she picked up the kettle.

"Did you want to come with me to a rehearsal?"

"Why would I want to do that?" said Eleanor.

"I thought it might give us something to talk about." He filled his mouth with the remains of the sandwich.

"Fuck. Dad. This is why I wanted to move out."

"Well, you are nineteen."

"What does that mean?" she said.

"Nothing." He shook his head. "Ignore me. I just promised a friend."

"And you promised me," said Eleanor.

"Yes, I know. But we didn't have anything specific planned."

"Like you would know. That was the point, Dad. Is it Georgina?"

"Yes," said Eric. Eleanor looked at him. "It's at the Am Dram Society in the village. I promise, I'll take you for lunch afterwards," said Eric. "But," continued Eric, "if we're going, we should probably leave."

———•———

"You really should part-exchange this, you know," said Eleanor of the burgundy car.

"It goes," he said, and sped off.

———•———

Georgina greeted them at the door of the village hall.

"This is Eleanor," said Eric.

"Nice to meet you." Georgina shook Eleanor's hand. "I'm Georgina." Eleanor looked at her.

"How's it going?" asked Eric. They followed her inside.

"Okay, I think." Georgina put a hand on her forehead. "We're changing things as we go."

"Can I use the toilet?" asked Eleanor.

"Yes. It's just over there," answered Georgina, and pointed.

"I forgot we were supposed to be spending the day together," said Eric.

"Oh, well, don't worry," smiled Georgina. "I'm pretty busy." They heard the voice of the director.

"Just stop there, please. Georgina? I think we need another line."

"Sit down. Here's a copy," she said. He watched as Georgina crossed the hall. In her absence Eric set apart two chairs.

"What's it about?" asked Eleanor.

"Well, I think it's just one act."

"What does that mean?" she said. Eleanor promptly took the script from him.

"All right, let's go through that again."

"Who's that?" asked Eleanor.

"Nigel," said Eric. "The director." They watched as the actors retook positions. Eleanor nudged Eric's shoulder.

"Mum wants us to come back for dinner," she said, looking up from her phone.

"Yes, all right," said Eric.

"That was good," said Nigel. "Really good. Shall we take a break? And consolidate what we've learned? Georgina?"

———•———

The Storyteller bit into some toast and then drew some pages towards him.

"How are you getting on?" asked Grace.

"Yes, good." He put the plate to one side. "I've got to the point where Eric is at Georgina's rehearsal."

"Did you speak to Max?" asked Grace. "You know he'll keep calling."

"Yes."

"I assume that means you haven't?"

"No." The Storyteller shook his head. Max was his editor. He hadn't told Max he was retiring. He thought he'd probably leave it until after the speech. It made it more difficult for him if people knew.

———•———

"What did you think?" Georgina asked Eleanor. "In the next scene the roles are reversed – but I don't think we'll get to that today. Eric," she said, "I was going to suggest we got a drink." She moved her head to one side.

"Do you ever tell us what's in the letter?" said Eleanor.

"No. I think it works better if we don't know. And that means I don't have to worry about it," Georgina smiled. "I'll text you," she said to Eric.

"I think it's going great." He looked at the stage.

"I guess we'll see," she smiled. Eric and Eleanor left the community hall to the sight of Georgina talking to Nigel.

"Did I ruin your day?" said Eleanor. Eric declined to answer.

18

"So," said Madeline, hurriedly tidying papers away from the table, "what did you two do today?"

"Dad introduced me to his girlfriend," said Eleanor.

"Did he?" replied Madeline.

"No, I didn't," said Eric. "She's a friend. We used to work together. She's rehearsing a play and I thought it would be interesting."

"Clever girl. You should hold on to her," said Madeline.

"He completely forgot," said Eleanor.

"Well, it sounds interesting," said Madeline. "Can you set the table, please?" she asked. "Who is she?" she questioned Eric. "Are you?"

"No," said Eric.

"It's ready," she called out. The sound of Eleanor's feet as they came down the stairs.

"Also, I thought we should talk about what she's doing. Now she's finished college and doesn't seem to have a plan."

"Yes," said Eric, nodding. "I had a similar conversation with Richard."

"Did you?" said Madeline. "What about your daughter?"

"Well, I was getting to that."

They sat around the table.

"Well, this is nice," said Madeline. "Does anyone want some wine?" she offered.

"Yes." Eleanor lifted her glass. "Definitely."

"Thanks," said Eric.

"So, what was Georgina's play about?" asked Madeline. The three ate and while they ate they talked about the play.

"I expect it's difficult to write a play," said Madeline.

"I could," said Eleanor.

"Then why don't you?" suggested Madeline.

"Dad's doing it."

"Are you?" said Madeline.

"Yes," said Eric.

"Like Georgina," said Eleanor.

———•———

"I thought it would be useful," said Madeline, "as we're here together. Listen to me," she said, "to discuss what you're going to do after college."

"I don't know," said Eleanor, putting a fork into her mouth.

"Well, do you want to go to university?" asked Madeline. "Your results were good."

"If I went," said Eleanor, "I would probably do a language."

"Shall we look into that?" said Madeline. "There's no harm doing the research."

"Okay," agreed Eleanor.

"That's all I wanted to ask. Just to make sure you're thinking about it."

"It's all we're thinking about, Mum. Richard's parents won't stop talking about it. They're neurotic."

"Well then, be grateful that we're not. Thank you for talking to us," said Madeline.

Eleanor took her plate to the sink.

"We still need to help her with the decision," said Madeline, as they washed up.

"Yes, I agree," said Eric, rotating a tea towel.

"But she needs support. She's only nineteen."

"Yes. I know," said Eric. He picked up another plate.

"How's she getting on here?" asked Eric.

"Fine. I think. I mean, I don't see her that much."

"We're not the greatest parents," said Eric.

"I disagree," said Madeline. "Look at everything we've given her." They carried the wine bottle and their glasses into the sitting room.

"The other thing I wanted to talk to you about, was us," said Madeline. Eric looked at her.

"What do you mean?" he said.

"I know I'm me. I'm too busy, and you're… But we still like each other, don't we? Enough to sleep together occasionally." Eric choked.

"I'm just asking you to think about it. We're only in our forties and neither of are seeing anyone. Are we? We're not really…"

"What?" said Eric.

"Enemies," said Madeline.

He slipped into the bathwater and pinched a cigarette between his lips, confident that the purpose of sleep was to keep the ghosts at bay. He then went downstairs. On TV was *Ideas After Dark*. Their special guest this evening was Dr Andrew Philpott.

"Good evening," said the programme's host. "We're very happy to have with us tonight Dr Andrew Philpott to discuss his latest TV series, *Object Lessons*.

"Andrew, objects are not the obvious subject for television?"

"No."

"Was the series difficult to make?"

"It only got made, I think, because of the other things I've done."

"Let me ask first, if I put it this way, how did you come to the subject of the object?"

"That's good, I'll use that. Erm, well, as I said, I usually take something ordinary and try to look at it differently. We interact with objects every day of our lives and it occurred to me that we never think about it; we only refer to them in a utility way."

"And what is that?"

"Oh, you know, as dispensable, ephemeral things. But in fact, they constitute an enormous part of our lives. The entirety of our lives actually. And this relationship, I don't think, has been properly explored."

"I think you'll need to explain that."

"Okay, well, we eat them in the form of food, obviously, and they are the materials from which we're made and from which we make things. But we do a lot more than that. Um, to make the point, for example, our museums are crammed full of objects the purpose of which is clearly not their utility. The relics and icons, I mean, through which our predecessors divined the workings of the world – the gods and monsters responsible for everything. And I don't think for a second that we modern people, if we are modern, have stopped using objects in that way. We're just not alert to it, as probably they weren't. Much, I think, to our disadvantage. I think this is something fundamental to our species. So, this got me thinking about a series that would look closely at it."

"Hence the title."

"Yes, exactly. Ultimately, I think a lot of good could come from it."

"At the beginning of the series you introduce the example of a shop that sells products with a mythical power to attract people."

"Yes."

"While the people making them are having an awful time."

"Yes."

"We know the people making them are having an awful time, but it doesn't stop us from acquiring them. Explain that."

"Yes, I mean, it's very simple, and I put it crudely, but the emotional reward they get from these fantastic objects is more important to them than the harm their production causes. The cultural appeal of these objects overrides our moral sense, is what I'm saying. The question is why? Why are we so disarmed?"

"And by 'these people' you mean, of course, us?"

"Oh yes."

"West and East?"

"West and East, yes."

"It's in the same territory as the nineteenth-century botanists who risked contracting every tropical disease going to discover a new type of flower."

"Yes. I mean, what is it we're getting out of it? It seems absurd looking at it under the spotlight of the studio. But we do it. This is our behaviour."

"We're chasing dreams."

"I am sure that's right. Incidentally, I think that ordinary descriptions like the one you've just used, 'chasing a dream', tell us a great deal. There is a fairly clear-sighted portrait of our psychology written into our common language if you choose to see it. We are undoubtedly pursuing some form of a dream at a tremendously high cost."

"Beauty in the eye of the beholder."

"Of an object, yes. I think you soon realise that our language is full of these insightful and often compressed descriptions."

"Is your point that this is a frequently told fact, whether we realise it or not?"

"Yes. You can say that about lots of things. It's just not something we want to reflect on, the reason being it can make things seem shallow, just behaviour. It helps me to make this point. That although in these examples we are talking about extremes, pathological obsessions, the relationship they have to their desired object is different only in degree, and not in kind, to the relationship we have with the objects we choose to surround ourselves with."

"Would you describe yourself this way? As an obsessive?"

"I have to say yes, but in the ordinary way. The objects of our desire need not be internationally prized works of art. They are most of the time routine objects, basic things such as, I don't know, the cup you prefer to have your tea in or a favourite brand of hair conditioner. They're the icons that feature in our most everyday rituals. Trusted brands. You're a Catholic. I prefer the baked beans in the blue wrapper.

Now, it's clear, just thinking about some examples, that how different cultures manage this psychological demand varies wildly, but the need to use objects in this way appears in everyone. If we're going to grow, then we need to grow from here. You can't duck it, if you see what I'm saying."

"It's tempting to hear this as part of the anti-capitalist movement; do you care to comment on that, at all?"

"Well, I really want to set that apart, to focus on this basic behaviour – the non-utility use of objects. It's not that I don't regard that movement as important, but my priority is simply the object. The magpie, as I've said, is of course another good folkloric example. In that, I find it faintly amusing that we mock the bird for collecting shiny objects for which it has no use, when that's what we do. 'It's just something the magpie does', but the magpie might say it's just something we do. A pattern of behaviour."

"I've had that experience of getting something that I'm certain will fulfil my heart's desire – only, in a short space of time to become completely disillusioned with it. Is that the sort of thing we're talking about?"

"Yes, exactly. I think it's a common feeling, and, again, it's extremely informative."

"Do you think the magpie gets disappointed?"

"Certainly."

"Do you get called a killjoy?"

"I do, sometimes, but I think if people really think about it, they'll probably appreciate what I'm saying. We all know, I think, that the products we consume take advantage of the fact that, for instance, our species finds colour attractive. We tend to think of that as shallow, when in actual fact it taps into something deep about our nature. This activity or sensory feedback is not, for example, something we switch on when we go to an art gallery and then switch off when we leave. There is no off switch. It's a permanent state and I think that's probably undeniable."

"Do you worry that if we give up the object, as you put it, then we'll suffer a profound loss?"

"No. My point is to just to do it better, Clive. If we understand what's going on, we can do it with less harm. Like I try and show, we get caught out by a sleight of hand that if it feels good then it is good. We're made to behave this way and we've been doing it for thousands of years. For example, it's natural for us to be awed by the architecture of kings. We don't react by turning away in disgust at the suffering caused to the people who, most likely of our own social rank, were forced to construct them. An unshakeable sensory appeal persuades us that behind the façade lies a moral authority. I can't suggest that we altogether revoke the situation, that would be foolhardy, we are who we are, and there are clearly good evolutionary reasons for linking together perception and pleasure. But I do feel it would be useful to expose its implications. It's about finding where the insight is, Clive, if just to recognise that we interact with objects for purposes above the narrow interest of utility. Such as, for the comforts of stability, permanence, continuity, order, safety. These instincts are extremely powerful. The success we've had at fashioning the world into its most comforting shape, goes a long way to disguise our behaviour. I happen to think this is why city people dislike the countryside."

"Dr Andrew Philpott, thank you very much."

"Thank you."

19

He had embarked on his first cigarette when he heard the letter box. What stood out was a hand-addressed envelope stamped with a prison address. He carried it with foreboding to the table and opened it.

Dear Eric,

Well, I didn't really have any friends and I wanted to write to someone, so I thought I would write to you – it was from David. Evening, day and night, in here, the only thing that anyone wants to talk about is why, why, why I torched the school. Disconcertingly (that's right isn't it? teach), the police, my solicitor, the prison psychologist – all of them. Nevertheless, I thought I would tell, tell, you, Mr Crawford. Even, I don't know if you know, but the car was damaged. So, I wasn't trying, you know, to kill you, murder you in cold blood. Don't know if anyone said? Anyway, it won't be Mum, and it won't be Dad. You wouldn't get anything from them. When I was born, they said I was the surprise boy. Eggs a woman has won't last that long, they told her, but they did. Doubtful then, I'd be made, 'Not-unwanted-just-unexpected', a blessing. No, I wasn't trying to kill you. Except it made me question if that was what I was trying to do. Such as I don't mind being here, should be, best be. Designated, as they tell me, a 'Cat C' prisoner – categorised. At least that means people like you can visit. Young people here leave me alone in general. Which is because, the staff tell me, they think I'm too weird. End of story. Don't you know why I'm here? No one is ready to say why they're here. Except I. Save me, the "Troubled David Spurling," who did the hard thing and opted out. Don't you have to choose what you want to be? Anyway, Sir, I'm going to continue my education in here. Yessirree.

Thanks,
David

Eric folded the page. He took the letter with him to lunch.

"I got a letter from David Spurling," he told Madeline.

"Right…" She took a sip of tea. "And why is he writing to you?" she asked.

"He wants me to help him."

"To do what?"

"Study, I think."

"At least he's thinking about his future. I assume he knows that you're a witness? You should hand it to the police."

"How should I respond?"

Madeline looked at him. "Well, how do you want to respond? What does your gut tell you? I would tell the college. Be transparent. Because these things have a funny way of …"

"Go on," said Eric.

"... of blowing up in your face. My advice is don't reply."

A young woman brought Madeline the pastry she'd ordered. "Thank you." Madeline then proceeded to cut it into pieces.

"If you feel you have to respond then think about it carefully. Send it to me. I'll look at it. Just consider what the college will think. I mean, it wouldn't look good, would it? And while we're on the subject of giving advice to young people, have you spoken to Eleanor?"

"Yes. Spanish. *Le gusta el español.*"

"And have you thought about what I said?"

"Yes," he said. "I'm thinking," said Eric.

"Okay." She checked her watch.

Eric took himself to the swimming pool.

Plunge.

1. The first breath always lasted the longest.
2. The bliss of your body weight lifted from your skeleton.
3. One length. Two lengths followed by three, and four.
4. He rinsed his shorts.
5. Having boarded the bus, he then walked up to the college. In a blue sky, strong winds pulled their cotton-white chariots. David's letter had started to burn in his pocket.

———•———

At work, he found Barbara waiting for him.

"Good morning, Eric, I wondered what time you got in. I've been thinking about your question," she said. At first, Eric didn't know what she was talking about. "About children and drawing abstract shapes? Why we generate abstract ideas is incompleteness," she said. "Do you follow? You were asking me about children. Surely, you've not forgotten? We need to know more than it's possible to know, so we invent. There isn't another answer," she smiled. Then hesitated with something separate. "You know I have a friend on the inside? Of the competition. I can ask him, if you like. If you wanted some advice," she said.

"Yes, that would be useful," said Eric. "How did you know?" he asked her.

"Georgina told me." She smiled.

"Right," said Eric.

"Don't be angry," said Barbara.

"I'm not," said Eric.

Eric ran his hand through his hair. Tina was quiet that afternoon. Sam made perfunctory comments. Perhaps it was no surprise. The rubble had gone, but that left behind a crater. Uncharacteristically for Sam, he had handed in a weak essay, as though he'd typed it out free-associatively. In the void loomed his play. So, he gave the seminar over to answering questions about it.

"What's it about?" asked Javid.

"Erm, well, it's about a school," said Eric.

"Like the college?"

"Yes. I send some students away to learn how to tell stories."

"We need a new story here," said Javid.

"Why did you enter?" asked Tina.

"A gut feeling," said Eric.

"Are you protesting?" said Sam.

"Erm, well, I suppose so," said Eric. It was either bewilderment or fatigue. He couldn't choose which. He took his tobacco pouch to the back door, wrapped in his bathrobe. A climate of convulsion. *A forlorn evening was like a stay in a strange hotel*, he thought. They were interviewing his mother again on TV. He sat down to watch.

"The safest countries have issues," said Francesca, generally.

"Yes, but I'm interested in why you asked for the charges to be dropped?"

"I think it's more important to find out why they did it."

"You're set to benefit enormously from the publicity, aren't you, Francesca Crawford?"

"Michael, that's too cynical a way of looking at it."

"Is it? Doesn't this move recoup the cost of the damage and varnish your image?"

"Money and the art world have always been in conflict."

"It's a bit late to realise that, isn't it?"

"Well, actually, I think it's something we have to be reminded of all the time. That in our society there are two systems of value. One prehistoric. The other is less than three hundred years old. If we put our culture behind a pay wall, then we put ourselves at grave risk."

"Isn't the bottom line that they damaged your paintings?"

"Maybe they've improved them, Michael."

"You went to see them in prison."

"Yes."

"How was that?"

"Illuminating."

"Did they hand you their manifesto, Francesca Crawford?"

"They were angry, and I can understand that."

"I see. Some people have reported that you're paying their legal bills. Are you?"

"I've made a small contribution."

"Isn't that absurd, Francesca Crawford?"

"No, I don't think so."

"This is a publicity stunt, surely?"

"Michael, I'm not going to agree with how you're framing this, however many times you make the suggestion."

"They assaulted you."

"Paint was thrown."

"It's well documented, Francesca Crawford, that as a young woman you lived an unconventional life."

"I think I've paid for that."

"And been paid for it, surely?"

"Michael," said Francesca.

"Isn't this the Francesca Crawford brand? An attempt to burnish your avant-garde credentials and in doing so expand your position in the market? I can hear the tills ringing."

"Would you ask Picasso that question?"

"No. But you're not Picasso, are you."

"Michael, you're suggesting that by offering help, I'm exploiting them – no. And what's wrong with my journey from one life to another? You started in regional TV. Should you have stayed there? You want me to concede that success is really failure? I think that's absurd."

"Some people say, Francesca, that when an artist's work finds its place in the market then its life as an artwork is over. It's just a commodity like sand and cement. What do you say to that?"

"I disagree. But it's true that money simplifies things."

"In that case, doesn't the truth get locked away behind a price tag?"

"If you like –" said Francesca.

20

The competition deadline is fast approaching. We don't want any of our applicants to miss out. So please take a look at our website for tips and support. We're really looking forward to seeing your work. Don't give up!

The best of luck.

Eric made breakfast and stood with a mug of hot coffee. Outside it continued to rain. A thick veil of cloud. He sipped the comforting liquid.

"Miriam?" he said, when it connected.

"Eric?" she replied.

"I've got a headache today and I feel awful. I'm sorry, but could you put a note on my door? And tell Jim. Yes. Yes, I'm sure I'll be fine, don't worry. Thanks. Thanks, bye." He put the receiver down.

By a quarter to one news that he was unwell had spread.

"I have a headache, but I'm not dying. How did you find out?" he asked Eleanor.

"I called your office," said Eleanor.

"Oh. Sorry. What did you want?"

"To use your computer."

"Sure," said Eric.

"For an application." She hung up her coat and sat down. She offered to make him a cup of tea.

"No, thanks," he said.

"Do you think she'll come, to your play?" she asked, meaning Francesca.

"I don't know," he said.

"Will you tell her?" asked Eleanor.

"I could leave that to you," said Eric. "I am sorry, you know. That you feel pushed to one side. You're not," he said.

"You've got to do what you've got to do," said Eleanor stoically.

"Yes," said Eric.

"Can I?" asked Eleanor.

"Yes." He nodded. "You know the password?"

"Yes."

"Why do you have all these things here?" she asked, stopping at the table.

"It's part of a puzzle," said Eric.

21

He opened his brolly and trudged along the pavement, fishing the keys out of his pocket. When the story felt more real to him than anything else, he felt good – he clutched the wheel – but when the real world took over, he didn't; the enterprise seemed immaterial. He got to the Larks' house and pressed the doorbell.

"Hi, Eric." Rebecca stepped aside to let him in.

"You got summoned, did you?" said Joe.

"Please be quiet," stressed Rebecca. Joe passed him with an armful of clutter.

"Is everything all right?"

"We've been arguing. Look," she said, "I need to ask a favour. Shall we?" she said. They stood beneath Eric's umbrella. "I was wondering if you'd take Alex to this exhibition he's been pestering us about in London. Get him out of here for a day, the way things are. I mentioned it to Eleanor." Rebecca's lips pulled against the cigarette. "We're struggling with a few things. I know it's probably not your preferred weekend, but you know he would love it if he went with you."

"All right," said Eric.

"Thank you," she said. She pulled on the cigarette again. "I know I rather forced you to say that."

"If it's Richard, you know he can speak to me," said Eric.

———•———

Joe came downstairs to join them.

"Here," said Rebecca.

"Thank you," said Joe. Eric and Joe's eyes connected for a second and then separated. They picked up cutlery and slid forks into their mouths.

"Well, I'll say it, shall I?" said Joe, looking at Rebecca. "We've got to sell the house. We can't afford the mortgage."

"I'm sorry," said Eric. "I imagine Richard, he'll be moving out though, soon, won't he?" Joe got up from the table.

"He's angry at me, but can't express it," said Rebecca. "You know then, I assume," she queried. "What decision he's made?"

"No," said Eric, and shook his head.

"I thought you would. You know I find myself now repeating what my parents said."

"Have you started looking?" asked Eric.

"For somewhere else? No," she said. "We haven't even told them. Or at least I haven't."

"It's just a house," said Eric.

"That's easy for you to say, isn't it?"

———•———

Rebecca Lark had the stage to herself, holding one of Eric's cigarettes.

"You can see. I suppose," she says. "The pressure." She looked about the hushed audience. "Who wants what, from whom? When?" She took a puff. "I don't know why I care," she smiled. "That's what Mum always used to say." She took another long pull. "I suppose we have to." Rebecca stood there in silence. Before emitting a curdled laugh. "Fuck it," she said.

———•———

Eric left. When he arrived home, he hung up his wet coat. He was pulled towards the table. The collection, which now had a space for David's letter. The small envelope plump on the oak top. He made himself a cup of tea and then afterwards came back to the table. He sipped. He'd been putting this off. Rubber tyres came to a stop at the kerb.

"Did you tell the police about the money?" Eric asked.

"No. Of course not. You've got nothing to worry about." He had to trust Richard.

"Well, don't tell anyone," said Eric.

"I won't."

"Okay." Looking at the table he had an irresistible urge to sweep it all into the bin. He was Eric Crawford. He lifted his eyes to the mirror, and then looked away again. The image a little too sharp. David Spurling drove a car at him. The yellow mask from the hospital lay on the table. The drugs they'd given Vincent, were causing symptoms of necrosis. He felt the scar from his appendix operation through his shirt. If he had any independence at all then it was in the shadows. He opened the back door and stood there. Freedom in the silent spaces. He saw the cigarette between his fingers as a tube of burning words.

"You know these spells?" the Storyteller said. "These pangs of nostalgia for old stories. I think we treat the problem with a natural question like, 'What colour is the sky?' You see how answering it places you in the here and now. It has anti-nostalgia effects."

"Yes," nodded Eric. "I think it's a good idea." But he found it difficult to concentrate.

The Storyteller took the sheet of paper out of the envelope, and sat reading it, silently. Then, once more, he took the book off the shelf. Flicking through the pages until he reached the part the letter quoted. It seemed that people liked doing that. Pointing out things to him in his books.

"'Some things exist only because there is a word for it'." True enough, he thought. Words did invent things. The Storyteller parted the pages.

"'Your father keeps complaining about a man in a forest.'

"'It's a recurring dream,' he told her.

"'Oh. I see,' she said.

"'All he needs is to be told it's a dream.'

"'I see.'

"'How is he otherwise?'

"'Oh, he's fine.' When he entered the room, his father asked him the perennial question.

"'I'm fine, Dad,' he said.

"'As long as you're happy.'

"'Tell me about the dream, Dad.'

"'It's just a dream. I shouldn't be afraid. It's just so vivid, I don't know where I am. You want to hear it?'

"'Yes, Dad. Tell me about the dream.' The thing was his father loved telling people about his dream.

"'Well,' he began, 'I follow this man into a forest. The path around us is banked high with snow.' His father raised a hand. 'As I watch, I realise,' he paused, 'that the man I'm following,' he paused again, 'is me. You know, sometimes like it is in a dream? You can be more than one person. The dark branches of the trees and the brilliance of the snow. It is sterile, but for one thing, the coat this man is wearing. All the colour and light in the world is trapped inside it. When it opens there is an explosion of colour, brighter than the sun. Where it is we're going, I don't know, but we go on for hours. The silence there is so silent that the rattle of the tree branches ring like percussive instruments. Out of his mouth clouds of steam rise. The 'he' that I am and the 'I' in my head, in this dream, that I am not. He stumbles and falls to the ground. Suddenly I know I am walking with him to death. The nimble frost gathers us. I watch him peer blankly upwards into the forest. The trunks of the trees are like gravestones. Down his legs/my legs/his legs, past his feet/my feet/his feet, to the trail we left behind. There, a gust of wind comes to inspect us. Far away there is a bird call. A sound that is hard to make sense of. We clutch our stomach. 'Are the rats here?' he says. Then a warm feeling spreads inside his coat. Abruptly he looks at the cuff. Out of it a small face appears. It is the round face of a wood nymph. 'When I am gone wear this coat.' He is repeating what his father told him. 'When I am gone wear this coat.' He is very afraid and throws the creature to the ground. He gathers his things and runs away into the forest.

"'That's when,' said his father, 'I usually wake up. Sometimes.'

"'It's a spooky dream, Dad. That's for sure. But try not to let it upset you.'

"'It doesn't really. It's just… I think I like it,' he said. He picked up his father's plastic cup and filled it with water.

"'Try and drink some water, Dad.'

"Language requires first an investment of faith," the Storyteller continued reading.

"When we look at ourselves represented in print what do we see? The symbol 'I'." *The Storyteller looked up.* "Maybe the convention does us no harm? But then again, doesn't he look a little shifty? Let's pick I off the street and rough him up. Wear him down with page after page of literature. 'Real, sir, are you? Or a figment of our imagination? Okay, okay. I'm a convenient symbol. I represent the bodily self, nothing else. I admit it, my usage got out of hand. But, in my defence, you don't say, do you, that no *I* is there, you say no*body* is there. I presumed you all knew that language was a tool for which misleading concessions were made.

"'And you, sir, lurking behind all these *he's* and *she's*. Come forward.' The third person omniscient narrator steps reluctantly out of the shadows.

"'And who are you when you're at home?'

"'I'm sorry,' says I. 'If it wasn't for me, they probably wouldn't have caught you.'

"'I'm nobody, really.'

"'Where do you live?'

"'I'm just a feature of the page, like him. But, if I may, I think, we've proven useful.'

"'How?'

"'It's comforting to have us around.'

"'Like gods and such,' says I.

"'To be fair to us, you do keep teaching your children.'

"'You really need to stop doing that if you want to stop thinking like oracles and such,' says I."

"Did you get all that?" the Storyteller said. "Language is a structure we throw off in our sleep."

"Yes," nodded Eric.

"Language is like a daydream. I'll say it," said the Storyteller. "We find ourselves in an unusual situation."

"Yes." The smoke from Eric's cigarette rose up to the flies. "At first I didn't really notice. And even when you do, it's easy to forget. You must have done something to change how it works. Made a decision or something," said Eric.

"Maybe." The Storyteller nodded, thinking about it.

"It puts us in an odd position," said Eric.

"I know I said it before," said the Storyteller, "but I'll say it again. We're just words, Eric. Just words."

"You're playing a part just like I am," said Eric.

"Something we didn't start, and we won't end," the Storyteller smiled. "A history to be combined and recombined in any way at all." The Storyteller picked up the letter. "No one is responsible, but everyone plays a part."

"That sounds like…"

"A play," completed the Storyteller. "I didn't write it. You didn't write it…" Both characters turn their heads. "Which means the author is out there somewhere. And it could be anyone."

"It could be everyone," said Eric.

"No one and everyone," said the Storyteller.

———•———

Eric stood.

The Storyteller sat at his desk.

"The next scene. I thought that, Georgina, you could read the next scene. Eric's next scene. In his play, I mean."

"Act 2, Scene 1," Eric interjected.

Storyteller: "It's hard to imagine…"

Storyteller: Looks down at his hands.

Storyteller: Looks up again.

Storyteller: "That it all comes from you."

Storyteller: "That is almost unbelievable."

22

"I'm sorry I couldn't stay the other day," Eric apologised.

"That's all right. I was busy," said Georgina. "Before I forget, I have these." She reached into her bag for two tickets. "I thought Eleanor might like to come?"

"I'll ask her," said Eric. "Have they contacted you?"

"Yes," nodded Georgina.

"What are they like?" asked Eric. This was the competition people.

"I don't know. Official," said Georgina. "I spoke to Barbara. She's excited."

"I didn't know you were friends?"

"Don't you have a soft spot for someone?"

Georgina's attention fell upon the seagull on the outside table gobbling up the left-over food with the chest pumped pomp and bluster of a general.

"I hate them," she said.

"It's our rubbish they're eating."

"I know I'm pathetic," said Georgina. "Do you think,

if someone transcribed our conversation you would be embarrassed?" she asked. "You know, like an automatic script. Wouldn't it be weird if, like in those sci-fi films, your imagination was a replicator? And every time you thought of your mother, another one appeared."

When she came back from the toilet, she put down two glasses in front of them. "Eric, if I suggested I came back to yours, would that be a bad idea?" she smiled. "I mean, I was just wondering if it was the time." *The chime rang on the Storyteller's clock.* Eric smiled. The two of them put on their coats. He showed Georgina to the bus stop. Then, when they got to his doorstep, he closed the umbrella.

"Oh, anything," said Georgina, when Eric mentioned what she wanted to drink. "Have you been here long, Eric?"

"Yes," he said.

"Can I put on some music?"

"Yes, of course." She delicately sorted through his records.

"Oh, I love this," she said, and set it down.

"Thanks." She took the drink. They stood together beside the sofa.

"It's a very nice house," she said, "expensive." She leant in and kissed him. "Maybe I could see the rest?"

She discovered Eric's accoutrements, when she used the bathroom, which made her smile. She was in Eric Crawford's house. While washing her hands she looked at herself in the mirror. If only Barbara could see.

"Hello. Did you want to go to bed?" she asked. He left his drink. She put a hand to his face. The sex was distinctly human. And Georgina, afterwards, she said, "Shouldn't we?"

Oh yes, of course, thought Eric. How could he have forgotten?

"I won't be a minute," he told her. "I'll bring it through."

"Act 2, Scene 1," said Eric. "It's an important announcement. It's about halfway," he said. He couldn't tell if he'd done this to take his mind off Madeline.

Georgina took the computer from his hands.

"Okay," she said.

Act 2, Scene 1: The Students Go Home

The students, Ryan, Charlie, Emma and Ivor sit side-by-side in the chapel. Ivor looked at Emma beside him with a 'Blank-blank' feeling about it. And then they all shared a 'Blank-blank' feeling. The feeling was something they didn't understand, because by education their emotions (which is where stories began) did not contain stories anymore.

"Why are they smiling?" *asked Ryan.*

"I don't know," *said Ivor. The others shrug.*

"Maybe they're happy?" *suggested Charlie.*

"Yes, I think it shows they're happy," *said Emma. They were all inclined to believe what Emma said, because she was clever. The faculty explained it to them in great detail what was going to happen.*

"What colour is the sky?" *said Charlie. They all looked out the window.*

"It's blue today," *they said. Ryan thought hard about something to say, because it still gave him a strange feeling to be silent.*

"I think it shows that they're happy," *said Ryan. But there was nothing anyone else could add and so no one said anything at all.*

"We're going back," *said Charlie. Their faces looked at him. Emma felt calm, and that made her only have a 'Blank-blank' feeling. And then because of Ryan's expression they all smiled, because it was still a convention to smile. People told the story of 'Yes' that way.*

"I'm feeling okay, today," *said Ryan. Because Ryan was prone to casting spells.*

Look! Look! Everyone turned to see. Here came the announcement they'd all been waiting for. This prompted Ryan's insides to wriggle with terrible excitement. He dug his thumb nail into his finger to stop a spell.

END of Act 2, Scene 1

"Eric," said Georgina, turning to him, "I think your story is very strange." Eric was silent. "Don't you think so?" she said.

"I think it's how it should be," said Eric.

"I like it." She nodded.

"Ivor and Emma go to work for The Office of Future Storytelling," Eric explained, "and they complete a story. It's a spectacular story."

"It's going to be performed at the college?" she asked. Eric nodded. Georgina looked at him, cradling the computer.

"I would drive you..." said Eric.

"That's all right," she smiled. "I'll get a taxi. I had a lovely evening."

"Me too." Eric nodded. "I'll see you on opening night," he said. They kissed, and then Georgina got dressed.

Eric watched Georgina get into the cab. Then he stood by the back door and inhaled a cigarette, gusts of damp air pushing him back. Eric sucked and flicked.

"You know," said Georgina, from the back of the cab, "that at this point I like to discuss something. I know that you have faith. And the text is a history that we share." Georgina looks to the right for a second. "Do you know the fairy tale of the girl in the castle? She's locked up by her brothers. All she wants is to be free. Her room in the tower is nothing to speak of. Its walls are bare, and the mattress she sleeps on is thin. But she has two things: a fire, and some books. After so much begrudging – she's been there so long she cannot remember – she takes a book and opens it. In spite of her resistance, she starts to read. In one of these books – maybe you'll think this is cruel, but it's true – she discovers a key. She clasps at it as her due reward. Her feet leave the bed, and she inserts it. Ready to taste her freedom, she turns the key, but instead of opening the door, all the key does is lock it. What good is the key? Sour for a while, the girl eventually goes back to her books. One day, as she's reading, she feels herself squinting, and a headache begin. The cause is the strong daylight coming in through the castle window. To her surprise, when she looks up, she sees that all the walls have disappeared. She appears in a park surrounded by people. All that she has, as a relic of her time in the castle, is the book in her hands."

Part Two

23

Act 2, Scene 2:

The Office of Future Storytelling

Ivor and Emma sit in The Office of Future Storytelling. Behind them is the City Administrator, Mr Merritt, and above him the Sector's top official, Mr Kind.

"Mr Merritt?" *calls down Mr Kind, holding a page.* "I was wondering if you'd read any of this? It's from that new one, Ivor."

"I can see that," *says Mr Merritt.*

"What do you think it means? He's writing some kind of fable about a girl who goes around the moon. Is that right, Mr Merritt?"

"Yes, that's right."

"Did we ask him to do that?"

"We asked him to write whatever he thinks we need."

"Right." *Mr Kind studies the page for a moment and then looks up.* "They're here to write something no one's read before. A new story of hope. Not easy. You required children with clear sight for that, not men crippled with nostalgia, drawn from the old cloth. So that was the problem." *He took a deep breath.* "And if you can't find the talent, you make it. Roll up your sleeves and you do the necessary. The point is to thrive, not just to survive. This is how I got installed in The Office of Future Storytelling. There is nothing romantic about it. It is just work. Good work. But work. You just want me to go on?" *He addresses someone off-stage.* "No, it's no bother at all." *He puts his hands together and collects his thoughts.* "Like new things their gestation is painful. But there's no need that I can see, or purpose served by raking it over. I'm certainly not rewarded for doing so, if that is what this is about. I'm just here to make sure things run smoothly, and they are running very smoothly. Our students come and they complete their shifts. Sometimes we send them out to gather information, because, you need to know your audience," *Mr Kind smiles.* "My right-hand man is Mr Merritt. He's Head of Operations, and a very good man he is too. Just a moment…

"Mr Merritt, I think we need to be careful with this." *He taps his finger on Ivor's page.*

At that moment a piece of scenery descends, which divides Mr Kind and Mr Merritt from Ivor and Emma downstage. Emma looks up.

"They took me," *she hesitated,* "home. Is that where they took you, Ivor?"

Ivor looked up and noded. "Yes," *he says.*

"Did you recognise it?" *she asked.*

"When I saw the front door, yes. I recognised it," *said Ivor.*

"Were there covers on the doors?" *she asked. In most cases their houses were boarded up.*

"Yes."

"But your parents, Ivor?"

"They were gone."

"They try and charm you," *she said.* "With their expressions. And so, you have to be careful. The people here."

They stand up and step forwards. Behind them a beach-side promenade with the audio of seagulls and waves. To their left there is an ice-cream stall.

"Would you like one, Ivor?" *asked Emma with new-fangled money in her hand.*

"Excuse me!" *the woman then said, as they were leaving.* "But are you two one of them, that's gonna tell us a story?" *They nodded.*

"Well, the best of luck to you," *she said.* "Bless you." *Emma licked the ice cream.*

"Did you get the bus today?"

"No," *said Ivor,* "I walked."

"I wrote that there were ten billion people on planet earth," *said Emma, licking her ice cream.*

"I wrote the moon got so close to the earth that it pulls away a piece of the ocean. And a girl gets swept up and goes around it in a river of sea water."

"What's her name?"

"I don't know," *said Ivor.*

"And is she a prophet?"

"No. She's just an ordinary person," *said Ivor. Then,* "I have to go," *he said, after a pause.* "I have an appointment to see my grandmother and father." *For a second their minds chimed with a 'Blank-blank' feeling.*

"What colour is the sky?" *asked Emma.*
"It's grey today," *said Ivor.*

Ivor met the sea on the corner. And from the window carried by the steady transition east, the right angle to the beach, saw the grassy edge of the cliff, and the sea colliding beneath it against a buttress of chalk. Ivor got down from the bus at the mouth of a narrow road, leaving it to carry on. Sparrows with short sharp calls, perched on wire fencing. The birds flew away. The bend of the trees in the wind, their smell, the empty field in a small shallow filled with long bending grass that moved just like the ocean, the fence posts rotten and the wire hung with a rust the colour of blood. He saw the pair of them. They were standing outside the house as though forced to abandon a place of safety. They had stayed behind, and it couldn't be clearer.

"I can't believe it," *said his grandmother as he approached.* "I could see you coming, but I couldn't believe it."

"What colour is the sky?" *asked Ivor, in the manner he had learned.*

"It's grey today." *Sylvia held her hands to her mouth.* "Will you come in?"

"I'd help," *said his father,* "but it's better if I don't." *Some days ago, he had seen his father on the wall outside their old house. He had a different expression then. He had coughed and looked as though he was trying to meet your eyes. You had thought he was going to say, he was sorry for having sent you away, but he cleared his throat instead, and said,* "I'm along the coast with your grandmother. I don't know if you remember…"

"What colour is the sky?"

"It's blue today," *his father said.* "Your grandmother would like you to come and see us." *His father stood up and lifted his collar.*

Sylvia brought in a pot of tea, which she hastily used to fill the cups, spout gently over the rim. Then she seized hers and put it to her lips.

"There," *she said, and smiled.* "I don't know what to say. Do you remember the house?" *She sipped hastily from the cup.* "What?" *she said, to her son, his father.* "I'm just saying how I feel." *Her hands were shaking.* "We went to that meeting," *she said.* "It was in an amazing building. The woman read to us, though I'm not saying I understood everything. But I'm pleased that we went. They said you were going to tell us a story. What kind of story is it?"

The scenery backdrop lifted. On the sheet of paper held in Mr Kind's hand were printed the words: 'You're All Going To The Moon.'

"Do you remember your grandfather and the bird?" *she said.* "The little bird you found in the churchyard. I think you were a bit afraid of it." *She smiled.* "Poor little thing. We showed it to your grandfather, do you remember?" *The memory opened like a flower, and for a moment Ivor was overtaken. It ran along the path in front of you. It launched itself in the church doorway. It struck the surface of the wall and then fell to the ground where it was dead. But it wasn't dead. It happened so many times that you thought it should be dead. In the end it let you take it without a fight. Tiny bird feet like wire and eyes that were black and shiny. He was having a feeling that was more than just a feeling. It was a story.*

His grandmother looked at him and his father. "Come into the kitchen," *she said, and stood up. She took the tin off the shelf.* "Would you like some? It's fresh. I made it yesterday. I'm going to have a bit." *She took plates from the shelf, cut it slowly and then lifted up the slices.*

"You see the vegetables." *She pointed through the window. She put the lid back on.* "Your dad. He did that."

"What's he doing?" *whispered his grandmother. She took a bite of the cake, rubbing her fingers together. They waited for him. But then they heard the sound of the back door.*

"Did we do something wrong?" *She put two fingers to her lips and licked them.*

His father was in time to see him board the bus. He turned his face into the wind. To the spray and air. He studied the water: the writhing of the turquoise marble patterns. He pulled the zipper of his jacket up to his throat. He put one foot in front of the other. His mother would worry if he didn't go back.

"Did you find him?" *she asked, as he closed the door.*

"I wasn't trying to find him. I just went out," *he said.*

She made him a cup of tea.

"He's got your hair. I remember the curls you had. Your father used to say they were as good as springs and we could sell them," *she said.*

"I know," *said Ivor's father. She put her hands together. Just once the little bird tried to escape. They had used the empty pastry box. But in the morning, when they opened it, it was really dead this time. On its side with its legs straight.*

END of Act 2, Scene 2

24

The sound of the alarm confused Eric. It was Saturday.

"Go on," said Rebecca, urging the boy inside. "Hi," she said. "Do you want anything?" she asked her son.

"A glass of water," said the boy. They left Alex to explore the living room.

"I need to talk to you," said Rebecca, as he filled the glass.

"Yes," nodded Eric, at the sink. He handed her the glass. Rebecca took it. They looked at one another.

"Morning, Dad," said Eleanor.

"Hello," said Rebecca warmly. "Your dad is on time. I put some lunch in his bag," she said. "So, Richard? He didn't want to come?"

"No," Eleanor shook her head.

"I'm sorry," said Rebecca, and hesitated. "Okay then, I'm going to leave. Have a good time," she said. "Bye!" she called from the door.

"You all right?" said Eric.

"Yeah. Are you?" Eleanor looked at her dad. "So, what's the plan then?"

"Well, you have a cup of tea, and then we'll get going." In the living room Eleanor found Alex inspecting his drawings.

"Why are they here?"

"I don't know. You'll have to ask my dad," said Eleanor.

"Are you ready?" said Eric.

They piled, the three of them, into the car, and then at the station passed their tickets through the machine. Then the slow clunky pull of the engine dragged them out of the station and set them clipping along the tracks.

"What is it we're going to see today, Alex?" asked Eric.

"It's about Stanley Robin," the boy said.

"And who's he?"

"He's a director, Dad," said Eleanor. "It's at the Moving Image Centre on the South Bank."

"Is film something you want to be involved in?"

"Maybe," shrugged Alex.

"You're just interested?" The boy nodded.

"Dad," said Eleanor, cautioning him.

"What?" Then he added, "Georgina's given us tickets for her opening night."

"Great," said Eleanor.

A woman with frizzy red hair sat down in the empty seat next to Eleanor.

"We're going to London," said Alex, looking up.

"Well," she smiled, "that's where I'm going, too. To see the Stanley Robin exhibition. I love his films. *The Mind Servant. The Tattooed Killer*," she quoted the titles. "But I'll tell you a true story. It's very 'Robin'. I was on the train last week and this man came on," she smiled at them. "And he looked like a toad," she grinned. "And he wore these headphones," she said. "Bright orange headphones. I've no idea what he was listening to, but he put out his tongue like this," she demonstrated.

"Oh, gross," said Eleanor.

"That's not it. First, he wiped it around his lips and then he began to shake. Then he opened a scrunched-up plastic bag and threw up."

"Gross!" Repeated Eleanor.

"He said it made him sick." Their frizzy-haired companion, Chloe Doors, was exactly right. The music made him sick. And it always had.

"What happened?" asked Eric.

"He got up. And he looked at me as though he was looking at everyone. And he said, 'It makes me sick!'," she said.

The man remembered that most important of days. His mother calling to him from the front door.

'I'm going to live in the music,' he told her.

'You're doing what? Are you making me chase after you?' Her hands were coated with flour.

'Come on,' she said. 'Come back.' But he had no intention of doing that. The music had sent him out from the record player, which his mother cursed, into the street, following that groove on the record. In other words, he was a very confused little boy. That was what his mother was thinking when, out of breath, she clamped her hands on him, and unable to say anything dragged him home. When she got her breath back, she did say something.

'Where the bloody hell do you think you were going?' It was the wrong thing to say to a boy like him.

"Anyway. I'm sorry," laughed Chloe Doors. "I'm a bit of a weirdo, myself." Their conversation ended and they were drawn to the sights outside the window.

———•———

They took the bridge across the river. He watched black and white video clips, while Alex and Eleanor went to see the props. When it came, the addition of colour, was garish like lipstick. He went for a solitary smoke. Or did he? He did, certainly, but, Eric, if memory serves, what you witnessed, wasn't that… *The murky green waters*. The interactive exhibits were the best. No, not that. *Across the waters, the skyline*. The deconstructed production, layer by layer. No. *The sight of the woman Chloe Doors?* Yes, that's it. Too much for him to behold. Eric put the cigarette to his lips and took a forceful drag. He'd taken the shortest glance. And a member of staff had used their arms to shield her from view. 'Please go straight to the exit, sir.' He'd looked this up. A copycat crime. She'd spread her excrement over the screen. She was giving herself to Stanley Robin. One advantage of dying at fifty-seven, they said, was that Stanley Robin had not had to witness this. Three weeks from now and the location would be Westminster Magistrates court to face charges of outraging public decency and criminal damage. It was captured on CCTV. She'd scattered sheets of paper. The message: 'Know that you love him'. For the moment though, all Eric had was the image of her holding up her hands, and the wide eyes of the security guard.

———•———

In the gift shop, Alex bought a *Tattooed Killer* T-shirt.

"Did you enjoy that?" asked Eric.

"It was awesome."

"You're not having anything?" said Eleanor. As they sat to eat.

"No, I'm all right, thanks," said Eric. He bought them hamburgers and shakes in the restaurant. Although he did end up eating some of their fries.

It seemed to him, as Eric gazed at the countryside, that they went up and down like metal horses.

———•———

"Come on, come in," ushered Joe. "Have you guys eaten?" he said. Joe put a beer in Eric's hand. "Tell me," enquired Joe, "did you see the sign outside?"

"Yes," nodded Eric.

"What do you say to Eric?" Rebecca said to Alex.

"Thank you," the boy smiled.

They went through to the patio. Joe and Rebecca had been working on the garden.

"Yes." She looked at it. "We're just planting a few new things to brighten it up. And hopefully they'll like it. How was it?"

"Good," said Eric.

Eleanor had gone upstairs to locate Richard.

"I'll see you tomorrow, and we'll go to my Dad's," she said.

"Yeah." Richard nodded from his bed.

"And you can print your application." Vincent was having his feet taken off. Richard had a bottle of beer on his bedside table. But none of it had been drunk.

"I'd better go," said Eleanor.

"Yeah."

"What's wrong?" asked Eleanor.

"Nothing," said Richard, looking away from her. He couldn't tell her yet.

"Okay. Tomorrow then," she said.

"Yeah." He nodded. She met Joe at the bottom of the stairs.

"They're outside," said Joe.

"Can we go?" said Eleanor.

———•———

A trace of streetlight rippled a course across the car bonnet.

"Thanks for coming," said Eric.

"That's okay." Eleanor shrugged.

"Have you thought any more about your course?"

"Yes."

"Because I know your mum's going to ask me."

"Why do we like them?" asked Eleanor, suddenly.

"They're old friends," said Eric.

"Why doesn't she buy her own cigarettes? She wouldn't smoke if you didn't smoke," said Eleanor.

"She got me into smoking, actually," said Eric.

"When you were at university? So, shouldn't you quit?" said Eleanor.

"Yes."

"You don't want to die, do you?"

"No," said Eric. They stopped outside Madeline's house. "Come over and watch a movie with me in the week?"

"Yeah. Okay." She nodded. "Night, Dad."

"Night," he said. He passed under the viaduct. Then made a split-second decision. He parked the car and walked up to the pub. He took a thirst-quenching, repressful mouthful. Then he took a notepad out of his jacket pocket. He ate and then, after they took his plate away, he went outside. He thought a little about rehearsals, but not much.

"Hello." His old teacher from when he was a student came up to surprise him. "I thought it was you. It's been a while," he smiled.

"It has."

"You're teaching?" he said.

"I am." Eric nodded. "Would you like a drink?"

"All right," his old teacher said. "You know," he smiled, "I don't hang around here waiting for old students to buy me drinks. They gave me a pension for that."

"I don't see why you wouldn't," smiled Eric.

"Thanks for this," his teacher said. "It's not the same job. I don't know how you cope." And then they got on to the obvious subject. "They're saying a student did it. Is that right? I never saw any of you lot being capable of that…" His old teacher raised his eyebrows.

"You must be grateful you retired?" said Eric.

"I feel very lucky," he smiled.

———•———

Eric woke up that morning to bright daylight. Then he registered the features of his living room. He pulled off the headphones. He got up. Then he walked back. It was Madeline he saw through the glass. He traipsed through the hallway and opened the door.

"Morning," said Madeline. "I get you up?" she said.

"What are you doing here?" asked Eric.

"I sent you a text. I thought we could just discuss things."

"Right." Eric ran a hand through his hair.

"You had a late night?" Madeline entered the house. "London not enough for you?"

"I went to the pub."

"Take a shower. I'll make you a coffee."

He got rid of Madeline with another promise. Then sat down to think about Ivor.

"Are you one of them who's going to save us?" *said the man behind the counter.* He put Ivor in a café. "Here's your tea. It's a pound. Thank you. Now tell me," *he said,* "do you know what's going to happen? Because here we've all been waiting a very long time. Oh, is that right? Is it indeed? Well, you'll enjoy that at least," *referring Ivor to the cup,* "I know you will." Eric scratched his face, and then continued typing. *Ivor carried the cup with him to the table.* This was, Eric checked his notes, Act 2, Scene 3. What he had titled, The Writer's Quest to Find Out?

A woman appears at the counter, just where Ivor had been the moment before. She is obviously nervous. She consults the rambunctious proprietor, who then points at Ivor. She then makes her way, between tables, to our hero.

"Hello. Is it Ivor?"

"Yes," *replied Ivor. The woman pulled back the chair and sat down.*

"They said you wanted to talk to me about what happened ten years ago?"

"Yes," *said Ivor.* "We need to find out what people were thinking. Why they protested."

"Okay. So, what do you want me to tell you?"

"If you could tell me exactly what happened? I think that would be very useful." *Ivor turned to a clean page in his notebook. The woman sat collecting her thoughts. She was divided.*

"I won't get into trouble, will I?" *she asked.*

"No," *said Ivor.* "Just think of us as a new set of eyes."

"Okay," *she said. And hesitated again.* "Well, I protested here," *she said,* "in the square. I came here with my boyfriend. Until the police broke us up."

"Why was that?"

"Umm. Because we thought Art was the greatest thing. The only thing." *Her voice sounded suddenly defiant.* "It's the best answer you can give," *she said.* "Isn't it? That you can't live without something. What can be better than that? And we were right, you know," *she said with defiance.* "We had a banner. It had a poet's name on it. It's how I got this," *she said, drawing attention to the scar on her temple.*

An elderly man at another table stood up shakily, and interrupted.

"You people! What are you dredging all this up again for? Call yourselves our servants? We've had it all and we've heard it all. The endless inquiries – why didn't we stop? Well, I'll tell, you. We all bloody knew what was going on, and we did nothing. *Nothing.* So, this is what we deserve. *No story.* It was always going to happen. We were always going to end up lost in the world." *The man pushed himself away from the table.* "There's no other way of telling it. You people, and your future – well look around you. *This is the future.* Ideology!" *He waved it away with his hand.*

"Well, you're doing great, aren't you!" *said the counter man, who began to laugh.* "You say I can't laugh? We had all of that."

"What did you do afterwards?" *asked Ivor.*

"Well," *the woman laced her fingers around the teacup,* "I supposed we just stopped talking about it."

"How would you describe that life?"

"Well, I thought it was like trying to live underwater actually. That's the best way I can put it." *She looked up, and then, as if startling herself,* "I'm sorry," *she said, and looked down.* "They said it would be all right, if we, if our eyes met. But I don't know. It's quite hard to get used to." *Ivor proved to her that it was all right now.*

In that space we go to another table where Ivor's fellow student,

Emma, sits. It is her turn. She's there with a woman in late middle age, who wears a mask.

"Do you mind if I take it off?"

"No," *said Emma*, "that's no problem."

She proceeded to unclip the mask and lay it on the table.

"You're still wearing it?" *said Emma*.

"Yes. It saved my life once. A lot of people," *she said*, "began to stare. Or they used to. I don't know if you know?"

"They're casting you in a dream." *Emma nodded.* "It was the model of satisfaction. The way people achieved meaning and pleasure back then."

"Oh," *she said, a little surprised.* "My," *she looked up for a moment*, "story. Is that what you call it?" *The proprietor put a cup of coffee on the table next to her elbow.*

"I was given shelter like this once, you know." *She looked around.* "You're looking at me," *she said*, "no one's done that for a long while. Not the way you're doing it."

"I'm sorry if it makes you feel uncomfortable."

"It does. But it's all right. If you're telling me it's all right."

"I want you to tell me what it was like to live back then."

"Well," *she hesitated*, "I wasn't born here. But I've lived here for a long time. I knew I looked good as a woman. A lot of people said so. I was encouraged, you know. And I did if I'm honest. That tells you all you need to know. They've got some idea in their head." *She looked across at Emma.* "You're a pretty thing," *she says*.

"We would call that an emotional story," *said Emma*.

"Right. We stopped anyway. Is that what you want to know, is it? What it was like?"

Emma sat calmly writing on her pad. "Yes," *she said*. "That's it exactly."

"The mask they gave us, that really helped." *She picked it up off the table and looked at it.* "That stopped it."

When she got home, she looked at herself in the mirror. But the conversation had left no trace. Her eyes looked just the same. Dark brown and blackish blue coated with a film of jelly. A fine ring of white all the way round the circumference of the iris. The fact that she had had to sit, and have it explained to her made her feel angry; or it gave her the story of anger. That's how she should say it.

END of Act 2, Scene 3

The work on the act was interrupted. A message he glanced at. It was to be Rebecca's moment. He set the work aside and made himself some lunch, before exiting for a quick walk. He sat himself by the old tree. And what was it that appeared? A bird. That busy creature. Out of some sort of exasperation he stood up, but the bird was gone.

People ran their dogs, wagging tongues and plumes of panted breath, in the mornings. But by one o'clock you were outnumbered by children in circles, boys punting footballs. He patrolled the prescribed paths, until the time came, hands in trouser pockets, where it was, suddenly, all roads led, to the house. For his friend Rebecca Lark.

"I'm sorry. I just went for a walk." He climbed the steps. She was there. "Everything all right?" he asked. He slotted his keys in and opened the door. "Did Richard say anything about college?" he asked. Rebecca didn't answer. Instead, she walked past him into the house. *So, is this it?* he thought.

"Would you like a drink?" he asked. She had coffee normally, thought Eric, as he filled the glass of water.

"Eric," she said, slowly. *Okay,* he thought, *here it comes.*

"I have to tell you this very boring thing," she began, and smiled. "You'll never believe it." But we and Eric, and everyone else, we believe. "You know how difficult it's been. My emotions are not under control. It's got the better of me. I've spoken to Joe and we both think it would be better," she said, "if we don't see each other. You've always been a good friend, but." She was making a mess of it. But, on the other hand, maybe she was getting it just right. She looked down at her hands. *You'd better get on with it, Rebecca.* "I guess that's what I'm trying to say."

"If there's something I can do?"

"No," smiled Rebecca, "there's not. He's been very good at not causing a fuss." At that moment they heard the front door.

"Hi, Dad," said Eleanor. "We're just here to use your computer to print Richard's form."

"You all right, Mum?" asked Richard.

"Yes," said Rebecca. "What are you doing?"

"We need to use Eric's computer."

"Great."

———•———

Eric and Rebecca listened to their children climb the stairs. She brushed a hand through her hair. With the presence of their children, she became acquainted with a different sense of the moment.

"What am I doing?" she said. "I'm mad." She looked at Eric through her fingers. "Our children are upstairs. And I'm —"

"Did you want to go out?"

"Yes." Rebecca nodded.

———•———

"How do you feel?" she asked Eric. "Did you ever…"

"Yes. I suppose so."

"I've thought about telling you," she said, "almost forever." They sat in silence beside the cycle track.

"Eleanor says she's having dinner with you," said Eric.

"I'd better get cooking then," she smiled. And then, "I just had to tell you. We've probably missed out on something, haven't we?" Rebecca said.

"Yes," said Eric.

"I wonder what would have happened if Madeline hadn't got pregnant? It's crazy. But we're human and this is what you think. Joe kept saying to me he didn't know why I'd started smoking again." She wanted to talk, and Eric did not want to stop her.

―――•―――

Eric sat down on the front step and rolled himself a cigarette. The sky now dusk. He checked his watch. He wondered if it was to do with an imbalance in the world. He skirted the outline of the rooftops. In the distance the trees in the park, the two merging. What had just happened was the reordering button. You learned it existed at the point you pressed it and the world exploded. Trees and houses all remained standing, people didn't die because of it, but there was still death.

"Eric?" interjected the Storyteller.

"Yes," said Eric.

"It's going to be all right."

"I'm not sure it is," said Eric.

"Why?" Eric looked at his cigarette.

"Well, I didn't think this was supposed to happen."

"What wasn't supposed to happen, Eric?"

"The category," he said.

"But it has to happen, Eric. Perhaps now you see the

difficulty?" he said. For the moment all they could consider was Rebecca. However hard the Storyteller tried – and he tried very hard.

"Should we just go there for a moment?" suggested the Storyteller. "Where our story wants us to go?"

"All right," said Eric, "but not for long." And so, the Storyteller it was and not Eric, who ran after her. When we catch up what do we see? Eyes that are rueful, sad, a face tight-lipped. A woman a regretfully short distance from home, but in need of her family. How much emotional ground there is to cover in such a short distance. How tightly reality gripped her in its arms. For once, Rebecca Lark hadn't fouled up. She'd done it. Reality would take care of that. She crossed the main road at the bottom of the park. The Victorian house came to her quickly. It couldn't possibly be a mirage, could it? Parked cars, trees and the leaves. She got there and watched her feet cover the chequered paving. To her almost surprise, she was happy.

"Are Richard and Eleanor here?"

"No," said Joe. She idled into the kitchen. "I think they're out." Joe bit into a carrot. She would allow Joe to fuck her that evening.

They didn't come for dinner.

"They treat this house like a hotel." Just a pleasant table for three then. He jerked and gasped. Twirling spaghetti on their forks and wiping their plates clean with buttered bread.

"I was thinking of getting a job."

"All right," he replied.

"Anything," she said. Joe acknowledged what she said but made nothing of it.

"You see how difficult it is," said the Storyteller. "Not to wish that this was a romance?" Eric nodded.

"You can't just throw it away. It's difficult," he repeated.

"There is only one way then," said Eric. The Storyteller listened to his character. "I write my play."

"Exactly." The writer moved a hand. "But even then," he said, "it will still be about love."

"Yes," said Eric.

"I'm sorry," the Storyteller confessed.

"That's all right," said Eric, throwing away an ember. "I had a feeling it was going to be like this."

25

Eric went for a swim to shake things out of his system. He had a desperately needed post-exercise fag, before scaling the stairs to his office. Then tipped a cold, discarded cup of tea into the plant as a substitute for water. Bowing to Barbara and her irrefutable logic he placed a call with her friend.

"Mr Birch? My name's Eric Crawford. I work with... Yes. Barbara. Yes. If you have the time that would be great. Okay, I'll send you something. All right. Okay. Thank you. Bye." This would get things on track.

He had a message on his phone from Madeline, which asked him cryptically, 'Is everything all right? X.'

'Yes,' he wrote back. 'Why?' Then he stuffed the phone back into his pocket.

26

They stood together on the college stage. They each had a copy of the script. Robert looked down at it. Where better to go over the script than in the location where it would be performed? He was a man about Eric's height, with pale and piercing eyes. After their phone call Robert had suggested he join Eric. Eric had found no argument.

"What do you think?" said Robert. "If you want to impress the judges this is the scene." He prodded the page.

"I'll get us some chairs."

They read it. Robert sat there holding his face for a moment.

"You see, for me, without your descriptive exposition it doesn't work," said Robert. "And that's a problem." He paused. "Barbara thought that because you're an English teacher, you might ignore the requirements of drama. Playwrights are not authors. And a play is not a text. It's an event. Your words are best thought of like that," he said, cupping his chin. Eric noticed, already, that Robert had a habit of doing that. "So, I would urge you to voice this essential narration through a character. Get it off the page." He lifted the page. "There's some good material. But… present it, is all I'm saying."

"What have we got back here?" Robert asked. "Are you stage managing it yourself? Have you thought about filmed material?" Robert held his face, again. "This is where the audience will be sitting? It's a good space."

Behind the curtain they looked through the equipment. The projector caught Robert's attention.

"There!" he said and pointed. "I'd use it. For all the difficult parts." He waved the script. "Here," he then said, pointing at some old props.

They spent an hour talking about how to dramatise it. How it should be performed. What to do and what not to do. At the end, Robert stood where he had started, on stage with his hands on his hips, as though they were about to start again.

"Have you cast it?"

"I'm doing that this week."

"Good." Robert surprised Eric then by handing him a tightly folded piece of paper. "Not before opening night," he said, and smiled, a sparkle in his eye. Robert put out his hand. "You'll be fine," he said.

Robert left Eric in the empty space. Eric watched as the older man exited through the doors. Their closing making a loud bang. He looked down at the pages of the script, but not to read them. To grasp instead the gravity of the undertaking. He locked the heavy doors. Dropping the script on the passenger seat.

———•———

In the kitchen, he poured himself a glass of orange juice. He then walked to the stairs.

"Eleanor?" He put a foot on the tread. Eric recoiled. He heard his play again. But the pair weren't reading it out dramatically; instead, it was like they were searching for something, a subtext. Eric's options were: 1 – leave the house to preserve their dignities, or: 2 – dive in. In the end he chose the latter.

The expression on Eleanor's face was appropriate. His presence in the room made them freeze. Eleanor in his chair and Richard beside her. *Eric watched as the ambulances parked up in the hospital bay and then took another puff.*

'We were just using your computer, Dad,' she said. Which was bullshit.

'But why were you reading my play? What's that got to do with it?'

'We wanted to see what it was about,' she said. He looked at Richard and saw no interest in the play.

'Well, you only had to ask,' he said. Eric played along for a moment. 'Is there something else?' He looked at their faces. 'Eleanor? Richard? Why are we standing here?' But perhaps he was aware already it wasn't going to end well. There was only one word and that word was Lark. He suddenly caught on to what was behind Madeline's text.

'We've got to go.' Eleanor shut the computer and picked up her bag.

'Eleanor,' said Eric. He moved to stop her. *One of those lucky punches*, reflected Eric. The gown they had put him in was part of the contract. He had lain by the door half hearing until the lights went out. He put it to his lips. He didn't know what happened afterwards. Who called the ambulance? Who else was called? He had no control. He guessed, of course, but since the blow to the head he'd had no permission to check. A lithe, young-looking sparrow scuttled beside the wheel arch of the parked ambulance. When he came to, the sight that greeted him was a woman with a swollen belly. He had been placed in an emergency adjunct to the maternity ward. She stared at him with bewilderment. Pull again on the cigarette. 'Mr Crawford? Everything is going to be all right.' Then he groaned and she, Lucille (the pregnant woman) said without alarm, 'I'll call the nurse.' Sinking, that was the feeling. It would take time to recover his former self. He took a moment. He was Eric Crawford. A teacher of English at Davenport College; he was writing, what? A play; his former partner was called Madeline, and his long-term friend, Rebecca Lark, had confessed she was in love with him. Yes, that was it. When exactly the innocent thing of a cigarette had persuaded her; what combination of words had opened up that closed shell and planted that idea? Or just a look, was it? A beam of light separating each precious crystalline strand of colour in the Catherine wheel of her eye. He didn't know. And how to decide? Yet Madeline, anyway, was coming. And anyway, something inside – he didn't know what exactly – pulled him together. Probably it was just these words.

"I'm sorry," she said when she arrived, "I got held up. How are you feeling?"

"All right. You?" he said.

She smiled. "I'm fine," said Madeline. There was the sound of a baby crying. "They couldn't have put you somewhere else?"

"Apparently not," said Eric.

"Maybe they thought you needed some mothering," said Madeline. "We were right, weren't we?" she proclaimed. *Madeline just knew everything.* "I imagine," she went on, "that

I am one of the few people for whom this isn't a surprise. Oh," she said, "the police have seized your computer."

"Why?" asked Eric. He didn't like that at all.

"Because of the circumstances," she said.

"And what are those?" asked Eric.

"I think Richard may have said something."

"Right."

"I have a computer you can borrow. I know you need one." A pause then. "They told me you're going home today," said Madeline. That was useful to know. "You can call me. If you want." Eric shook his head. "No, it's fine. I'll call a cab."

"Why do you think this happened now?" asked Madeline. "And not before? Before she had the boys. I hope you realise Rebecca Lark is incapable. As someone who has loved you," she said. "I can tell you she doesn't have it. And by that, I mean what you need. I've watched you for long enough. We all have. She's unhappy, but you're not. It did take me a few years to understand that," said Madeline. "Anyway, I hope you'll be able to forgive them. I brought you some clothes. If you need something, give me a call. I think your trial starts here, Eric," she said.

"Thanks."

"That's all right. What are friends for?"

"Are they going to charge him?" Eric asked suddenly. Stitching it together.

"I don't know," she said. "He put you in hospital."

———•———

Eric got dressed. Completed the paperwork at the front desk. Freedom came with fear. He got out of the lift. The sky cloud-white. The flow of patients and professionals in and out of the automated doors. He checked his watch. This was where he'd watched the clowns. Now he was a clown. Christ. It wasn't raining outside, but the air was chill. Time elapsed. Eric checked for a cab, looked about aimlessly, deliberated and with a deep breath opted to propel himself.

He walked down through the car park, between the pedestrian white lines, to join the world of healthy people. Behind the perimeter wall was a busy road, cars and lane-clogging buses, and the sprawl of the unplanned, and ungovernable, city. He conceded, for now only to himself, that he should have awarded the people in it the correct attention.

The pavement side and the high wall convinced you that the hospital didn't exist. A weight in his pocket alerted him, which a slipped-in hand revealed to be his phone and headphones. Madeline was clever. He looked up at the seagulls skoonering and he realised that somehow, he was always coming back to the hospital. He plugged his ears one by one. He thought about what people were saying, while casually plotting the pedestrian course. Before the first junction by the traffic lights there was the sixties flint courthouse – he would be there for David's trial. The dour journeymen who stood outside in typically grey suits seemed to recognise him. The black eye? But maybe they were telling him as well, that he was off the rails.

An armada of packed buses swept by. The occasional passer-by did a double take. On account of his proximity to the pool a dangerous impulse to swim. He paced out to the edge and dove in. The best thing about water is that it can take the weight of the world. He swam to the end, touched the side and continued swimming. On the ninth or tenth length his left goggle filled with blood. A rosy colouration, a gentle pink hue. When he took the goggles off thicker blood fell into the water. The sight of ribbons. A lifeguard called him out. A few screams. They applied first aid, deciding in the end to call an ambulance. Eric's efforts to explain were rendered mute. There was no choice. He explained his complicated story to the doctor. The doctor listened patiently as she inspected his eye.

"Sorry," she apologised for hurting him. "Why did you think this was a good idea?"

"I just wanted to swim," he said.

"Right." She nodded. "Because the goggles have split the skin. So you'll need stitches. The swelling is the problem. Nurse?" She carefully stitched the skin back into place, applying finally a thick cream. She asked him, as the equipment was tidied away, a question.

"Mr Crawford. Are we going to be seeing you again today? Or can we send you home safely?"

———•———

Outside Eric rolled with jittery fingers a cigarette. There he was again. No energy left for thinking. Wait, restraint – as the traffic went by. He held on to a plastic bag which contained his new swimming clothes. At the park, he stopped to look at a fallen tree, like a whale lying there on a shore. Two hundred and twenty-two steps completed the distance to the front door. On impact a mausoleum-feel, and muddy bootprints left behind by the paramedics. He made himself a cup of tea and sat with it. The silence was benign. The steam rising, mistily, he took a pen off the shelf.

27

Monday morning with a black eye was not an enviable prospect. Of course, everyone was going to ask him what happened, which in the terms of common human currency they had every right to. There were tutorials all morning. The last with Tina.

Tina: "Fuck. What happened to you?" she said when she saw him.
Eric: "I got punched in the face?" He couldn't be bothered to deflect or argue another case.
Tina: "By who?"
Eric: "My daughter's boyfriend."
Tina: "Shit. And I thought my parents were… Why?" she asked.
Eric: "It's complicated."
Tina: "You screwed up."
Eric: Demurred.
Tina: "It's not often that someone, such as I, witnesses

the decline of one of the paragons of the academic establishment."

Eric: Looked at Tina.
Eric: "Shall we discuss your essay?"
Tina: "Did you fight back?"
Eric: "No."
Eric: "I was knocked unconscious and spent the weekend in hospital."
Tina: "Fuck." She laughed and apologised.
Eric: "Shall we discuss your essay?"
Eric: "Despite your obvious pleasure at my misfortune, I think it's excellent. Novel and perceptive. Well written. Well argued. You should be very proud of it."
Tina: "Thanks."
Tina: Silenced for the moment.
Tina: "You don't have amnesia? You're definitely talking about my essay?"
Eric: "Yes. I marked it before this happened." Eric pointed at his eye.
Tina: Nodded.
Tina: "So, what's your next move?"
Eric: "What do you mean?"
Tina: "With this?"
Eric: "There is no move."
Eric: "What are you going to do?"
Tina: "I thought I would work on the subject more."
Tina: "Do you need a drink?"

She was going to do well in a world that didn't offer second chances, thought Eric.

Eric: "Yes, all right." The rightness or wrongness didn't seem to matter anymore.

"I'm not sure I should be telling you any of this," Eric told Tina when they met in the pub.

"Well, you don't have to tell me," said Tina. "You can say whatever you like. I'm not going to tell anyone."

"So, what did you do? To deserve that?" she asked.

"I'll tell you a story," said Eric. Eric told her the truth.

"Why did you give him a thousand pounds?" asked Tina.

"I thought it was the right thing to do."

"Was it?"

"I don't know," said Eric. "Probably not. I mean, it didn't help in the end."

"Every few months they change her drugs." They spoke a little about Tina's mother. "She gets better, for a while, and then it's back to how things were."

"You handle it well."

"Why should I give up? I'll go back if I have to." She pulled open the packet of crisps. Tina then asked Eric about how he became a teacher.

"I did my degree."

"You like it, don't you?"

"It suits me."

"You were young," she said. She munched a handful of crisps. "Like, my age."

"Yes, almost." Eric nodded.

"Your mum's Francesca Crawford."

"Yes," he confirmed.

"What's that like?"

"Awkward, mainly. I lived with my grandparents. Not far from here. A sister," said Eric. "She travels with my mother. I don't envy her."

"What about your ex?" Tina chewed. That was a good question.

28

Madeline. Today she was the sound of the sea reaching the shore. Madeline held her hands inside her pockets as her feet sank through the pebbles down to join him on the sand flats. Daylight in her eyes. Eric had contrived this just for her.

"I told Eleanor I'm going." She meant to the night of his play.

"Is there any news?" he asked.

"About?" asked Madeline.

"I don't know, anything?" He had brought Madeline to the sea because that made them close. Neap tide was the time of day to grant you access to the rock pools. Beyond smooth sand, tide-scoured stones, clumps of seaweed and the litter of the odd crab shell or deceased dog shark. On a clear afternoon – as this was – the wet sand carried an astonishing reflection of the sky. A mirror planted under the chin of the world.

Tiny streams of water trickled beside their feet. When they had lived together on Clermont Road, they would come down whenever the winds were strong. And there watch big waves crash. Or at low tide to watch the wading birds. These were groups of pink-legged oystercatchers or black-billed egrets, dipping to feed on crustaceans. So, what made it appropriate to bring Madeline was easy. Did Eric miss it? Well, at the moment how could he not?

"These guys are brave," said Madeline, referring to the kite surfers.

"Yes."

"Eleanor's not coming," said Madeline, "to the play. I'm sorry." Eric was under the assumption that he didn't have time. "Don't underestimate the idea that your parents might get back together," she said. Then she added, "Joe called to say Rebecca's moved in with her sister."

"Why did he do that?" Eric asked.

"So that I would tell you," said Madeline. "You know the process, do you? For court," she asked.

By the time they climbed to the top of the beach the sky was orange.

They'd bought the house together with his advanced inheritance. He was the youngest teacher at Davenport College by a country mile.

"You know you should think about quitting," she said, referring to the smoking.

"Yes." Eric nodded, without putting up any kind of fight.

"The good news," said Madeline, "is that Eleanor's submitted her application."

"She probably wants to get away," said Eric.

"I will try and tell her none of this is your fault." Madeline looked at him.

"Thanks," said Eric. "I'm grateful for that."

"I know," said Madeline.

29

1. Eric completed the final draft and stood by the back door to the chug-chugging sound of the printer. When it finished, he collected the pages and set them in a folder, which he set on the table. He was tempted to call Eleanor, but doubted himself.
2. On Monday morning, he delivered the manuscript to the cast. Latham called him, so, he explained the format. Leaving it until the last moment to say that his mother was coming. Eleanor's efforts at persuasion had been successful.
3. Eric stood at the back door.
4. In truth, this cleared the way for David's trial. There were other staff, not just him, called to give evidence. With it an understandable degree of nervousness about the impact it could have on their jobs. But everyone knew that it was essential.

30

The flint-encrusted building. Eric arrived dressed in a smart blue suit. He was checked with a wand and then directed up a flight of stairs. A volunteer led him to a private room. A copy of his statement arrived, which he read through.

"There is no telling," said the volunteer, "when you'll be required." Half an hour, and the barrister entered.

"Eric Crawford? Hello," he greeted Eric, "I'm Daniel Proctor, for the prosecution. I'm so sorry to have kept you. The good news, I hope, is that we've been able to agree your evidence, which means the defence no longer wishes to cross-examine you. You don't need to take the stand. But I must thank you for attending. Without witnesses we don't have cases," he smiled. So, Eric handed him his statement and in place of the witness stand took to the public gallery.

The case of the student who blew up the college. It had obviously attracted attention. Most of the seats above the court were occupied. Eric found one at the very back. The scene should be imagined as a conventional English court room. Oak, Queen's coat of arms, barristers in black frocks and horsehair wigs, an obligation to stand whenever one spoke, and language polished by the ages. The presiding judge in David's case was His Honour Judge Jay Wycombe. A man of grey curls, renowned for feasting on every scrap of legal plankton that floated before him. It was in this world that Eric found himself. Miss Baxter, the advocate defending David, addressed His Honour.

"This puts me in an invidious position, Your Honour, not to be able to cross-examine the witness on this basis. Might I say in response to my learned friend's argument" – gestures to Mr Proctor – "that a sliding scale in this case may be a slippery slope. That prevented from making reference to prior events in this young man's life I may be unable to defend him."

"Do you wish to submit legal argument, Miss Baxter?" asked the judge.

Miss Baxter hesitated before demurring.

"Your Honour, no."

"Well then, let's proceed, shall we? The next witness?"

"Mr Kevin Quail, the janitor, Your Honour," said Mr Proctor.

"Let's have Mr Kevin Quail, then, please," said the judge.

Mr Proctor was a tall youngish man with wig plumage a light-brown colour. While Miss Baxter, by contrast, was a little older, with plumage a little darker. She possessed a clear and defined voice, which gave her an assertive air in the courtroom.

"Mr Quail," asked Mr Proctor, "can you tell the court your role at the college and who was due to clean Block C at Davenport College on the evening of Wednesday the 6th of May?"

"I'm the college janitor and it was David Spurling."

"And whose signature is it on the rota for that time slot?"

"David's."

"Mr Spurling's signature," the barrister repeated. "Could anyone else have had access to the building?"

"Yyyesss. But they would need to know how to get in."

"Would they need a key?"

"Yes."

"Does the log sheet show anyone else present?"

"No. David would have known that."

"Make sure you just answer my question, Mr Quail. You said he would know. Why is that?"

"Because he's cleaning the building."

"I see. How likely would it be, in your opinion, as the defence have suggested, that someone else entered the building that evening?"

"Quite unlikely."

"Quite unlikely. To your knowledge no one else was either in or entered the building?"

"No."

"Mr Quail, thank you. If you could wait there, there will be some further questions." Miss Baxter rose to her feet.

"Mr Quail. The evening of Wednesday the 6th of May was Open Day, was it not?"

"Yes."

"So, there would have been a lot of people at the college?"

"Yes."

"I have no further questions, Your Honour."

Judge Wycombe called the court to rise for a short break. Eric left the gallery. He studied some barristers. Cars went by on the road.

"I want you to stay there," the Storyteller stressed. Eric nodded.

"All parties for the trial of Spurling!" It was now time for David to take the stand. We watch as David reads the oath.

"I do solemnly, sincerely and truly declare and affirm that the evidence I shall give shall be the truth the whole truth and nothing but the truth."

Miss Baxter walked them through the evidence. She pointed out its weaknesses. There was easy access to the college and ample opportunity for someone else, other than David, to have opened the gas taps. The jury had to be sure, beyond any reasonable doubt, that the prosecution's case was correct, and that no one else but David could have committed the act.

It went well for Miss Baxter. Her arguments, put with her controlled tone, were incisive. It was unfortunate, therefore, about the interruption. The ill-timed kind. A creature of adventurous habit with feathers and feet, not made timid by formal matters, up on high from a fractured windowpane.

"Madam Clerk, we have a guest," said the judge dryly.

———•———

"No, that's not it. The unexpected thing…"
"I'm looking back on it," said Eric.
"All right," said the Storyteller.

———•———

The court staff dealt with the bird while they sat on the soft chairs in the public corridor. Then they got back to it, with Mr Proctor holding the floor.

"The suggestion that someone else is responsible for this is just pure fiction. We have a letter in our possession sent by you, Mr Spurling, to your former teacher in which you admit that the explosion was part of some sort of 'lifestyle choice'. The prosecution regards this letter as tantamount to a confession. It's on page thirty," he directed the judge. "Is this letter a confession, Mr Spurling?"

"They used that letter," Eric told Madeline. She called him to find out how it went.

"I did tell you," she said. "So, do you need to go back?"

"Yes."

"What's that for?"

"Something called a *voir dire*."

"A trial within a trial," she said, surprised, "and what's it for?"

"Well, it's for me," said Eric.

David looked down at a photocopy of the letter.

"It was collected by the police. As it should have been. Mr Crawford is a witness in this case." David's face produced a flash of anger.

"You're required to answer the question," prompted the judge.

"No," said David.

"No, what?" asked the judge.

"It's not a confession."

"Let me read it to you," offered the prosecutor. "From line twenty-one."

'Don't you know why I'm here? No one is ready to say why they're here. Except I. Save me, the "Troubled David Spurling," who did the hard thing and opted out. Don't you have to choose what you want to be?'

Mr Proctor took off his glasses.

"What did you mean by that?"

"Not what it sounds like."

"And what does it sound like?"

"Like I'm saying I meant it."

"Are you saying you did it, but didn't mean to? Because that is no distinction."

David laughed.

"If you have something to say, say it," interrupted the judge.

"No. I didn't do it."

"Very well. But then what does it mean?"

"It's just something you say."

"You're telling us that what you've written is a fantasy?" queried Mr Proctor. "Why were you saying these things, Mr Spurling?"

"I don't know." David shrugged.

"Perhaps you can help us with this. The police seized your computer, is that correct?"

"Yes."

"And in analysis of your activity, they found this, which I identify as Exhibit 'K'. It is a statement you uploaded to the website of an organisation, which the public have grown to know, I'm sure, as the protest organisation called, 'The Wednesday Group'."

"Mr Proctor, is this of probative value?" asked the judge.

"It goes to possible motive, Your Honour."

"If there are no objections?"

"None, Your Honour," said Miss Baxter, standing and then sitting.

"Mr Spurling," asked Mr Proctor, "what is The Wednesday Group?"

"It's an action group."

"For what purpose?"

"To protest."

"To protest against what?"

"The future will be decided by how we choose to make meaning in the world."

"The future will be decided by how we choose to make meaning in the world," repeated Mr Proctor. "Let me read out what it is you uploaded so that the jury and court can hear it. It's Exhibit 'Q', on page forty-two, Your Honour. Mr Proctor cleared his throat.

They tell us what to think,
And we think it,
Repeating their mantras over breakfast and sometimes sociably just for fun.
And they like that,
Because it's money in the bank,
An extra element of control over how we spend.
The force,
Taken lightly,
The Think Box they've put us in.
Oddly we do not recognise,
How strange is the situation.
We do this all for free,
Out of some curious and unexplained loyalty.
Think thoughts for someone else's benefit,
Not seeming to think that it is old-fashioned labour,
That we're still working,

Churning it out,
The Think Box they've put us in.

"Mr Spurling, I put it to you that causing the explosion to C Block at Davenport College on the evening of Wednesday the 6th of May was a premeditated political act. You thought about it, planned it, and executed it."

"No," said David.

"Your Honour, I have no further questions." Mr Proctor sat down.

"Miss Baxter?" said the judge.

"Your Honour, I think this matter can be simply put. Mr Spurling, was the letter you wrote to Mr Crawford related to the prior incident involving Mr Crawford, in the Davenport College carpark?"

"Your Honour," interrupts Mr Proctor, "the relationship between the accused and Mr Crawford has no bearing on this case."

"Yes," said the judge.

David let out a laugh.

"Does that laugh conceal a point?" the judge asked.

And then came the surprise we'd been waiting for.

"Mr Crawford told me to do it," said David.

Silence filled the courtroom.

———•———

"But you didn't, did you," said Madeline.
"No. Of course I didn't," said Eric.

———•———

"I require you to repeat your last remark," said the judge.

"And you're absolutely certain of that, are you?" The eyes of the judge turned to Miss Baxter. "Direct identification does not form part of your client's defence. As a result of this new evidence, I think we must ask the court to rise and you address me *in camera.*"

In camera

"Your Honour," said Mr Proctor. "Mr Crawford has been sitting in the public gallery. His evidence was agreed this morning. It is far too late for the defence to be raising this defence."

"Is there any merit to this assertion?"

"Your Honour, no," said Miss Baxter. "Not on the evidence."

"Miss Baxter, do you wish to cross-examine Mr Crawford?"

"No, Your Honour, I would suspect not. I seek instead a moment to speak to my client."

"I see no way forward other than to discharge the jury," said the judge. "The jury has just heard evidence from your client contrary to both your defence and the existing evidence. You're beholden by your client's instructions and they have changed from lack of ID to a defence of coercion, bribery, joint enterprise, and who knows what. Surely this makes it impossible for you to agree Mr Crawford's account and a fresh trial is necessary?"

"Your Honour, as you know well, ID is often the defendant's preferred defence where the truth of the matter is that the offence was committed under duress," said Miss Baxter.

"Then surely you would wish the police to investigate for duress?"

"Your Honour, on my feet, before a decision is made, on the basis that this has been a well-investigated case, my question is whether it would satisfy the court if a *voir dire* were conducted in respect of Mr Crawford's evidence to determine whether it comes up to proof. A *prima facie* test, in the absence of any actual evidence that would cast doubt on Mr Crawford's account. In short, Your Honour, to rule out this line of defence."

"The bar has already agreed Mr Crawford's evidence," said the judge.

"Well, Your Honour, precisely."

"What basis is there to cross-examine this witness?"

"Your Honour, the simple test that the court determine the value of his evidence."

"And as we expect, if it does?"

"In those circumstances, Your Honour, I would consider asking Your Honour to instruct the jury to disregard my client's remark. A regretful outburst by a young man facing a lengthy jail sentence."

The judge considered the situation. "You can have twenty minutes. When we return, I want clear direction. If this trial is going to stop, I want it to do so immediately."

———•———

Eric stood outside.

"Mr Crawford? Could I speak to you for a moment?" the police officer approached him.

"Yes." Eric nodded. DC Bradbury took out his notebook.

———•———

"You know, it's entirely feasible that these issues crop up," said Madeline, "clients change their instructions and wrong-foot their advocates all the time. It's often a complete illusion you know what's going on."

———•———

"Your Honour," Miss Baxter addressed the judge, "I am pleased to tell the court that the time it allowed has been put to good use. I have spoken with my client about his evidence. I have also spoken with my learned friend" – hand gesture to Mr Proctor – "and the officer in the case. I would like to thank both for their assistance. The position of the bar, Your Honour, is this: that a *voir dire* be sought to address the point of law raised with Your Honour *in camera*."

"Is the bar happy with that position?" the judge asked, looking at both their faces.

"Your Honour, yes," nodded Mr Proctor, lifting himself up from the bench.

"Might I remind your client that fabricating a defence is a very serious matter. Have you warned your client, Miss Baxter, about misleading the court?"

"I have, Your Honour. On behalf of my client, I would like to apologise for the disruption. It is, however, right and proper that all aspects of this case are considered."

"Well, I agree, but I expect that to have been done before the trial," said the judge.

"Your Honour, yes."

"I adjourn this matter until tomorrow, for a *voir dire*. All witnesses on standby."

As the court rose, Eric met David's eyes.

"It's to ask you some questions," said the officer, blithely.

"I can't tell you any more than that, I'm afraid. But Daniel will lead you through it tomorrow."

———•———

Eric stood before his front door to unlock it. If they put the teacher in the dock that would make for an avant-garde defence. He put his keys down, loosened his tie. After he'd finished his call with Madeline he ran and sat in the bath. The octagonal glass balanced on his chest. "*Voir dire*," he repeated, taking a sip. No point in anything except the truth.

Eric picked a book from the bathroom floor, pinched the cover and spread the pages. The Storyteller found they read it together. Aptly it was about a man in a terrible predicament.

"He displayed no aptitude for business," it began. "He wasn't interested in the mechanics of what had delivered him to his social rank. He was interested only in the future. After his father's and two brothers' deaths, it was left to the employees to buoy the enterprise. The shock of nineteenth-century mourning. After it dissipated, on a dank and drizzly afternoon, a gaggle of clerks came looking for Joseph. Sir Charles Aubrey, his father, until his sudden violent death, had been a wily industrialist. One, unfortunately, with a disinclination towards friendship. It had become clear, in the months leading up to his death, that the other mills were streamlining. Placing Aubrey's under pressure. And the banks that had once so eagerly lent them money were becoming hesitant. Now there was no Sir Charles Aubrey, nor his preferred heirs, Edward or Thomas, just Joseph, their demands for repayment accelerated. Joseph sat with his fists on his father's desk —

"You don't mind, do you? If we continue a little?"

"No," said Eric.

"The staff were so accustomed to the iron grip that his father had on the business that they kept important things to themselves. More weeks went by. Their stock sinking as fast as their ships. There had been a spate of storms which had caught several of Aubrey's vessels in the seas around Africa. Stupidly, perhaps, it had not occurred to Joseph that the business he now led could send men to their deaths. His mood began to swim in these dark waters. As he had done before, when faced with difficulty, he reached out for fiction. He just loved it, being taken away by a story.

"In April, in fear of reprisal, he sent his wife, Katherine, and his mother to seaside lodgings. He sent Katherine lonely letters. 'The gates through which horses used to pull my father's carriages, are silent. No one comes here anymore, except to make demands. I so wish this nightmare would end.' Joseph had a romantic streak. The reality of course was that Katherine, and his mother, were looking for alternative suitors amongst the gentry.

"The book Joseph loved at the moment, was called *The Cavalier*. It contained sentences like: 'Carmela sat with her husband as he wrote down his testament, under the watchful eyes of the soldiers. His hands slow, and deliberate, the nobility which, all along, had been his power. "My darling." He looked up at her, with visions of the soldiers' livery. "Don't be too long." And she put her hand on his to strengthen him.' If only there could have been some of that for Joseph.

"In the months to come he was to discover, however, that his world was not without a chink of light. Just as things seemed to be at their worst, Joseph discovered something, or a more exact way of putting it was that he discovered someone. Those thunderous clackety-clack machines, which his father had spent so much time with, held a secret. Despite it having been their combined weight that had splintered the beams, 'As anyone,' they said afterwards, 'could have told you,' he now found through them that he understood. Combine it with a retooled habit and Joseph could rightfully feel that the fate of Aubrey's Linen was not so bleak. Let us explain. On meeting anyone he had always dashed off a description. 'A juvenile habit,' his father called it. Writing down who they were and what they were, just like the succinct character descriptions that appeared in the books he loved. He'd done this for comfort before. But now in the recesses of his mind, a germination took place. Meeting their retinue of bankers, creditors, and lawyers, he was surprised when one afternoon he found himself not to be surprised. The same day, when he sat at his desk to commit further to his record, he was again surprised that there was nothing to add; he knew these people better than he knew himself. He gazed at the fire, uncertain of what he was thinking. His mind flipping the situation over, like a coin. It went on like this a little while, until the insight suddenly woke him. That bead of light. The child of this invigorated state was an idea that would change his life and the world forever: people, he thought, were just like those murderous machines. The days he sat through of debate about cost and economic theory, he could set aside. For the pitch he was listening to was concomitant with his new mode of calculus. He converted the idiosyncratic habit into a set of scores for guile, evasion, misstatement, and in reverse, honesty, consistency and truth. In short, he was turning the novels he had read and the habit he had formed into a thirst for information. Once he had deployed it, the people he dealt with didn't fail to recognise, rather uneasily, the peculiar gift Joseph had for anticipation. Luck would also play its part. A problem with the machines took Joseph one day into his father's factory. Ending up right where it was that his father had insisted on taking his brothers. He realised quickly that he'd misunderstood the purpose of his father's visits. There he came across a man, whose name he'd never forget, called Arthur Wren.

"'Took your time, didn't you?' Joseph noticed how his clerks did not intervene to rebuke the man for his impertinence. In their hesitation there was again something all had known but had been too timid to say.

"'Might we talk for a moment?' said Joseph.

"'Come into my office,' Arthur smiled. The two clerks stepped forwards.

"'I'd leave them behind if I were you,' said Arthur. 'Your father and I, we always spoke in private.' Joseph did as Arthur Wren suggested.

"'The way your father and I did things was based on frankness.' Arthur laced his hands together and tapped the tips of his thumbs. 'He would tell me what the problem was, and I would tell him what I thought the answer might be. I'm not one for wasting time, and neither, I'm sure you'd agree, was he.'

"'We need to cut costs and increase profits,' said Joseph.

"'Yes,' smiled Arthur.

"'How would you suggest we do that?'

"'What is it that we ship?'

"'Linen,' said Joseph.

"'And what do we ship back?' asked Arthur, unstacking and setting three small wooden cups on the table.

"'Spice, sugar and rice' said Joseph. Arthur looked up.

"'No,' he said. 'Would you like to try again?' Arthur pulled a book off his shelf, removed a piece of paper and unfolded it. On the page was a diagram of one of their ships. Arthur put his finger down on a compartment in the aft section.

"'What's this for?' He studied Joseph's reaction.

"'I don't know,' said Joseph.

"'Your father's stones,' he said. Without waiting for Joseph's response, he asked a more direct question.

"'Do you know a man called George Cedar?'

"'No,' he didn't.

"'Then you don't know your father's business,' concluded Arthur abruptly. His father's business, Joseph learned, was founded on a loan from a London jeweller, called George Cedar, who as part of their agreement had demanded that the debt Sir Charles owed him be repaid in stones. The rare and the less rare kind, which required his ships to sail through rougher seas to ports in Africa, adding danger and three weeks' extra duration to each trip. Added to the time was the weight. The weight meant they sailed more ships, which was fine when you dominated the market, but it was a massive disadvantage when you didn't. The space they required for the stones prevented him carrying more profitable crops, like their spices. 'Pay off that debt, convert your ships. And listen,' said Arthur, 'whatever Cedar tells you, ignore him. You are not your father. Understand?'."

"Mr Crawford," Mr Proctor addressed him, "we thank you for returning to court today. Miss Baxter and I have had the opportunity overnight to review the evidence. We have prepared a list of questions on the basis that you coerced David into releasing mains gas on the 6th of May. Your Honour, you will see that the prosecution has found it necessary, under their disclosure obligations to serve further material. You should have received a new bundle?"

"Yes, I have," nodded the judge.

"I'm grateful, Your Honour. Mr Crawford, this has involved us taking a look at all of the evidence in connection with you, is that clear? DC Bradbury has, I trust, reminded you, that at this time you are under no caution or suspicion for this offence. Is that correct, Mr Crawford? You remain exclusively a witness in this case. I'm going to start with the statement you made to the police in May, before moving to the letter you received from Mr Spurling, and then the wider evidence. In your statement you set out your whereabouts on the night of the explosion. This account has been checked by the police. And so therefore I don't intend to ask you any more about it. What myself and my learned friend Miss Baxter are interested in, is your relationship with the defendant and any motivation you may have had for coercing him. When asked about your relationship with Mr Spurling, you have stated that you didn't have one, but for the prior incident in the car park. This was approximately three months prior to the gas explosion. Is that right?"

"Yes, it was."

"This involved Mr Spurling losing control of his parents' car which nearly collided with you."

"Yes."

"And you've explained this as entirely out of the blue."

"You had never met Mr Spurling before this incident."

"Due to the facts of this matter, you were first on scene. Is that correct? You called the ambulance. You went with Mr Spurling to hospital. Where you stayed with Mr Spurling until his parents arrived. Is that correct? How many hours before his parents arrived? Enough time for you to build up a rapport if one didn't already exist?"

"I see. How long were you with David at the hospital while he was conscious?"

"And what did you talk about?"

"Nothing else?"

"Nothing else at all?"

"Is it fair to say you were the only familiar adult present?"

"Did you build a relationship of trust with Mr Spurling at the hospital?"

"Mr Crawford, do you know why the incident in the car park occurred?"

"How do you explain it?"

"It could have been anyone?"

"What about the letter? Why did David send you the letter?"

"And there is no other reason for that? Nothing in the history between you?"

"Mr Crawford, you wouldn't have been seeking revenge, would you?"

"You understand I have to ask each and every pertinent question. Mr Crawford, we understand you're writing a play. A number of your colleagues mentioned it in their statements. It's being performed in two weeks. Is that right? The officer in the case, DC Bradbury, has made us aware of a recent incident at your home. One for which you received that cut around your eye. At the same time your computer was seized. And we have a copy of your play here. Your Honour, do you have a copy?"

"Yes. I've read it. Very interesting, it is."

"You explore the manipulation of children. Were you manipulating David as research?"

"Mr Proctor," interrupted the judge.

"Your Honour, I would hope that you appreciate why the bar are asking Mr Crawford these questions? It's an opportunity for Mr Crawford to deny these claims."

"Not in the present case. Miss Baxter?" the judge invited the defence barrister.

"Your Honour, thank you. Mr Crawford, I echo my learned friend's remarks in respect of your attendance today. Erm, do you expect us to believe that the incident involving the car and the explosion at the college, both involving my client, both involving you, are unconnected?"

"Miss Baxter, careful, please. Mr Crawford is not on trial here."

"Your Honour, my apologies. Mr Crawford, I spoke with my client yesterday. And we discussed the remarks he made. He made a number of further claims, which I think it's important I put to you. You knew that David had a fascination with you. True or untrue?"

"Miss Baxter, what are you saying?"

"Your Honour, my question is to be understood in plain terms."

"Very well."

"Mr Crawford, in plain terms, were you aware of this? My client said that he made numerous attempts to obtain a place on your English course. Is that true — ?

"No? No recollection of that at all?"

"My understanding is that it was against his parents' wishes," said Eric.

"Has your client lodged a complaint of any kind with the college?" asked the judge.

"Your Honour, I don't know. I would have to check with the officer in the case."

"Mr Proctor?"

"Yes, Your Honour."

"Have records been obtained from Davenport College?"

"Your Honour, no. We don't have the college records. As Your Honour knows, the defence of duress was not raised and so therefore no effort has been made to investigate it."

"Well then, let me remind you, Miss Baxter, that the purpose of this hearing is to test whether Mr Crawford's evidence comes up to standard. Not to use it to make further allegations. If duress is your client's defence, then I can only insist that it be properly investigated, which means we discharge the jury. Miss Baxter, are we clear about this?"

"Your Honour, yes. If I may I just have two further questions. Mr Crawford, is it true that you invited my client to your birthday party where you instructed him to release mains gas at C Block at Davenport college?"

"No," said Eric.

"Have you ever been an active member of The Wednesday Group?"

"No," said Eric.

"I have no further questions. Does Your Honour have any questions?"

"No."

"Mr Crawford, I will end this by wishing you good luck."

———•———

"How did it go?" asked Madeline. She sat on her sofa with the phone to her ear.

"The jury came back with a unanimous verdict," said Eric, "of guilty."

"Well, that's no surprise, is it?" said Madeline, adjusting her feet.

"They grilled me," said Eric

"You would expect your advocate to fight for you."

"Yes," said Eric. "But this was like fiction."

"It's a rare opportunity to test people. At least it's over now, Eric, and you can move forwards. I imagine you're all keen to do that."

"Yes," said Eric.

"Get a good night's sleep. You'll feel different in the morning."

"I expect you're right."

"Goodnight."

Part Three

31

From a difficult night's sleep through to the moment you woke up. The day of the play, and what a day. The more so because you were alone, no one to talk to, and no distractions. Fingers and thumbs; lean against the back door. What to do with time? Would you have gone through with it? Silly question; of course you would. Eric turned to us with the cigarette between his fingers, the light from the window reflected on his glasses. But he didn't say a word.

Francesca got into the back seat of the car to collect Sofia, before joining the motorway southwards.

"Are you excited?" she asked, as Sofia sat down. "To see your brother's play?"

"Yes. Are you?" said Sofia, looking at Francesca.

"Of course," said Francesca. "Has he written anything like this before?"

"Not that I know of," said Sofia.

Eric sat at the table with lunch on a plate, surrounded by his curios, along with a tattered copy of the script.

Puckered pages, scribbled notes, as useful as a rabbit's foot. He showered, masturbated, and then went for a walk. Still, it was only three o'clock. Hours yet to go. He sat down at the park café's plastic table, eyeballed the newspaper, ordered a coffee. Quite naturally the news today did not hold his attention.

He watched the families play. The odd insect. A bee go by.

When he left the park, it was to walk home. To sit on the sofa to flickering television images. He chose the blue suit again, with a white open-neck shirt. Picked up the script, collected his keys, turned off the lights and shut the door.

Behind the safety of the windshield, he watched as people attended the performance. A steady stream of people entering the college through the school gates. He took hold of his courage and got out to join the guests. How light and empty did he feel. The simple thing was that the play was to be performed. Police officers were positioned about the school grounds presumably on account of his mother. He didn't know who was responsible for organising that – Latham, he suspected – which proved to give the evening a certain edge.

"Hi," he said to the police officer as he entered the hall. The inside was a bit like a puritan church, with a mezzanine floor and a balustrade around the upper section, coming to a stop beside the stage curtains. The main seating area was on the floor, where he sat on his chair, fifth on the third row.

"Hello, Eric," said Georgina. He looked up. She wore a yellow dress. "Here?" she queried.

"Yes." He nodded. He found it difficult to take his eyes off her.

"Hello," smiled Georgina.

"Madeline," said Madeline, shaking Georgina's hand. Madeline sat the other side, wearing a scarlet suit. "I heard about your play," said Madeline.

"Yes," smiled Georgina. People knew she was already into the finals at the end of the year.

"I don't think I can avoid asking," Georgina said, turning to meet Eric's eye. "About your eye?"

"What? Oh, this?" he said. "A misunderstanding." She nodded courteously.

"Do you have the script?" asked Georgina.

"Yes," said Eric. He produced it from his jacket and handed it to her.

"I like to follow," said Georgina. That reminded him of Robert's note. It had said simply, 'Enjoy it, Eric.' He'd opened it in the shelter of his jacket.

"Where's Eleanor?" asked Georgina.

"She's not coming," said Eric. Georgina looked at Eric.

"Right," she said. Speculation could take her no further.

To the left of Georgina, Adrian, his mother's driver. To Adrian's left, Sofia, his sister, and at the very end, on the corner seat, beside Sofia, the guest of honour in all but name, Francesca.

"Hello, Eric," she'd said to him. "How are you?" He'd said back, "Yes fine."

"Not too nervous, I hope?"

"No." From there, nothing. The six waited as the hall filled with mothers and fathers, students, and his colleagues. All but for five seats, that is, that he'd reserved for Eleanor and the Larks, on which Eric focused his attention.

Watching the play proved to be a kind of hallucination; listening to Ivor's ice-cream monologue; peering at Mr Brain's newspaper; scenes tumbling. The Second Act, and his young prophets became writers, getting to the point, and then what were they waiting for? 'The Story of the Future'. He glimpsed Georgina turning the script. Adrian, Madeline, his mother; their concentration. At the final interval, he went outside. He thought he was alone, but it proved not to be so.

"Can I have one?" said Sofia.

"Yes," he said, and looked down at his shoes.

"How are you?" she asked.

"All right. Francesca?" he asked.

"Oh, she's fine," said Sofia and exhaled.

"I didn't know you smoked?" Eric told her.

"I don't usually. Only in England."

"Are you seeing anyone?" he asked.

"No," she said lightly, and shook her head.

"Your own work?" She demurred.

"What do you think of the play?" he asked.

"It's good," she said.

———•———

So finally, it came to the last act. It began with a close-up of a woman giving birth. The future, as it always had, began with a child. A few mutterings of disapproval made Eric question their choice of footage.

Act 3, Scene 1: The Story of the Future

"It is expected that in the next hour Marianna Rapiz, from Puerto Rico, will give birth to the world's ten billionth person. You'll know, if you've been watching, that we've been discussing the implications of this milestone birth with our experts, but now let's go to our reporter, Carol Kroll, live at the public video screen. Carol, we're not far away, are we?"

"Good evening, everybody. Not at all. I'm at the Royal Square with three members of the public to find out what they think about this landmark birth. Charlotte, you first, please?"

"I think it's remarkable." (*Reporter nods.*) "But it's important we remember this is a child just like any other child, and deserves to be received with the same joy as any child."

"A valid point. Mark?"

"I share what Charlotte says, but there is this bigger picture."

"Ten billion is a lot of people."

"It is."

"Liam. You?"

"No doubt it's a milestone in all sorts of ways. On the one hand it's a baby, and we were all babies once, but there is this unavoidable number. Ten billion. It's a shocking number. And we can't be blasé about it. There will be more of us tomorrow and more of us the day after. People are genuinely concerned with what it means. I think we feel it on an intuitive level, and that's why people are at the screening, to find out, because we really don't know. I also think Marianna is going to make a ton of money out of this."

"Thank you, Liam. If I can direct our attention to the screen, I'm sure you've got a clearer picture in the studio, we can see that Marianna is heavily dilated – I'm not sure if I would have chosen to give birth on TV – but you can really see the head, our first glimpse of Marianna's baby girl. She's still unnamed. Mum says she wants to 'look her in the eyes' before naming her. Charlotte, give me your reaction to these pictures."

"Well, it's just very emotional. Such a profound experience for a woman. I have two children, and it takes me right back to when they were born and I was in hospital, fighting for their lives. It happens all the time, but it's unique to you."

"Mark? And your reaction?"

"Oh, I think everyone can feel it. You can tell by the quiet of the crowd, it's very pregnant, if I can use the pun."

"You just about can. Erm, I'm hearing in my ear that given the amount of dilation, we should expect to see the baby within the next thirty minutes. We know from our studio paediatrician, Dr Leslie Campbell, who's been monitoring Marianna's pregnancy for us, that there are no complications. The baby descended correctly to the birth canal, and so in a matter of minutes we should all be listening to the child's first cries. For the moment though, we're going back to the studio for some other news."

"Thanks, Carol. Astrophysicists have recorded that the moon has moved closer to the earth. Scientist Hilary Scott told this programme earlier that, 'at such a scale small changes are big changes,' and would have an impact on tidal behaviour. No one at this stage, other than the freight and fishing industries, should be concerned. 'The path of the moon is known to fluctuate. But scientists are at pains to explain the recent shift.' We now go back to our main story. Dr Leslie Campbell, where are we?"

"Well, we can see" (*she points at the live video feed*) "that Marianna is fully dilated, and the baby's head has crowned. We can see the nurses and the doctors, giving her maximum support. That's the baby's father, Victor, I think, the plain-clothed gentleman to her right. We need the next push from Marianna to be big and powerful. The midwives will want the baby to be out as soon as possible. Here's the baby's head, which is fantastic, and look, here come the shoulders as well, textbook and a great relief for everyone."

"Live to Carol, Carol?"

"There is a huge reaction, everyone around me is cheering, and many people are weeping and hugging each other. And, as I'm speaking, we have the baby's cries, ringing out across the square. Lots of happy people, a memorable day for everyone. Not least Marianna. I'm sure it's going to be a very busy couple of days."

END of Act 3, Scene 1

Act 3, Scene 2: One Week Later

"Dr Hilary Scott, do we now need to reclassify the power of collective consciousness?"

"I think that is a very good question. I think that we do. It has completely caught the scientific community off guard that there exists this natural law, which inadvertently or unknowingly has been discovered. I think we do now need to treat the collective consciousness as a physical law like gravity, with a real causal effect on objects."

"How do you respond to the suggestion that the level of consciousness can be reduced with medication?"

"I really can't comment on that. I can only talk to you about physics. The moon's current position is startling, and we really are speechless. The likelihood, based on the moon's position, is that within the year a proportion of the earth's oceans will orbit the moon. When did anyone think they would say that?"

"That is why people are arguing that death row criminals should be executed."

"I'm not here to offer comment on political issues."

Three Weeks Later

"The breaking news this evening is that 'Sky Water' has carried a young woman to the moon. Her journey is being tracked, but all attempts at interception have failed. Frantic efforts are underway to piece together what has happened. We have been told to ask for anyone who may have witnessed anything in connection with these events to come forward. Now, to discuss the situation, our special guests tonight are the Reverend Morris from Montclef, astrophysicist Dr Hilary Scott, and broadsheet journalist Gregory Dunn."

"Reverend, let me start with you. What do you make of this?"

"The only thing that can explain these events is God, God, God. The scientific community has no answer."

"Reverend, you have a theory, I believe, that our ancient churches are dormant technology with a secret purpose for the future."

"I absolutely do, yes."

"What do you think that is?"

"I have absolutely no idea. And why would I? But I do believe that they're completely unexplored technology."

"Is that related to this event?"

"I couldn't tell you, but I wouldn't be surprised if it was. Change is upon our race."

"Dr Scott. To you next. What is the opinion of the scientific community?"

"Well, we've seen one important rule be broken, why not another? I think we're trying to keep an open mind. We don't know what the new lunar conditions are, so I don't think we can rule out the possibility that this woman will survive."

"Gregory Dunn?"

"If collective consciousness can attract the moon to the earth, why can't it protect a woman who goes to the moon? It's possible that the human collective is protecting her as we speak. In effect, it could well mean that we sent her. That seems to me an effective, albeit startling reading of the situation. The question then is why did we send her? Was this situation inevitable? I don't know. No one does, including the Reverend Morris."

"You're suggesting that we're all protecting this woman?"

"Yes, I think so."

"For some purpose, Gregory Dunn?"

"Yes, and that doesn't need to be mystical. It could just be regulatory. An intrinsic regulation of physical forces."

"Doctor, is that all it takes to protect someone? Just the operation of our minds?"

"It's possible, but we can't be certain."

"I see you're sticking to that line. Reverend?"

"It's obvious, isn't it? This is the impact of prayer. Why has the moon moved? We did it together. Why did we do it? Is not in our hands. A time for faith."

"Could there be other thresholds that we don't know about, Dr Hilary? That we could inadvertently stumble across?"

"Yes, absolutely."

"And let me ask all of you: what does it mean for our political leaders? Should we be demanding elections? Gregory Dunn?"

"I would hope for that to be the case. We must have elections in the wake of such events. Our leaders must present us with a manifesto for a new age. Ever since the birth of that child I have been thinking to myself that we are not what we thought we were. It is a sobering and releasing thought, actually. We have got to look at everything very carefully. And to be frank with you, I find myself thinking thoughts that I never thought I would – I am sorry for getting emotional, but that's the truth. I lament what has happened and because of it, I hope."

"Well, that, I think, is a perfect place to stop. No doubt we'll be coming back to this. Thank you to all of my guests. We live in remarkable times."

END of Act 3, Scene 2

Act 3, Scene 3: The Young Woman Who Went to the Moon

Narrator: "Olivia was, I guess, the odd one. We were old enough to have jobs, but too young to know where we were going. Money to spend but no money, if you know what I mean. That Friday, well, we went out as usual. Why we liked the place so much was because you could overhear other people's conversations, like the most sociable bar in the world."

Supporting cast: "Hear! Hear!" *The lights go up, revealing an animated bar. Glasses are raised and toasts are given, before quickly subsiding.*

Narrator: "We were just talking like we usually did. Guy, Luke, Olivia and myself. Olivia was talking to us about the behaviour of our bodies. If we knew what the weakest part of them was. If we knew, even though we were young, what was going to kill us. I know that sounds miserable, but it wasn't. I'm sure we spoke about other things, but that is what I remember. A heart could be too strong and pump in the blood too quickly, for instance. Guy said something stupid like he usually did."

Guy: "It's true. I did. I said, 'I know what the strongest part of me is!' But we were young."

Narrator: "Patrick and Louise, Olivia's sister and boyfriend, left us. So it was just the four of us. And the 'Sky Water', of course. But no one knew yet what to think about it."

Guy, Olivia & Luke: *Each of them nods in agreement.*

Narrator: "We just got on with our lives. I knew that Olivia had been to the video screen, something like a month before, for the birth of that miracle baby. It was all over the news. It was difficult to miss. It was a big deal, but that's all we thought. We didn't realise it was going to change our lives forever."

Narrator: "'That number will just get too big one day.' said Olivia. 'Well, if we can't manage our resources any better,' I said. But then who really knew? And that was it. They were just normal thoughts coming from normal people. In the end we decided to leave the bar."

Guy: "It was my idea."

Luke: "Was it?"

Guy: "Yes, it was."

Luke: "I thought it was my idea? That we should go to the park?"

Narrator: "I see now that the ordinary can have extraordinary consequences. We bought some cans of beer. Which *was* Guy's idea."

Guy: "That was my idea."

Narrator: "So, we went out into the night. The sky was a dark blue. And the moon it seemed was just huge, like if you wanted to you could touch it."

The bar staging was rolled away. In its place a park and in the sky a large bright yellowish moon. Downstage, the four of them, the Narrator, Guy, Luke and Olivia, pick up beer cans, and with them the story.

Narrator: "Right in the middle of the park, surrounded by flat grass. Trees stood like guards. We shared out the cans and opened them with a loud click and a frothing fizz and drank. Guy and Luke then hatched their joke."

Luke: "I think this might be my fault," *he confessed, can in hand.* "I definitely think I enabled it."

Guy: "Who did you enable?"

Luke: "You."

Guy: "That's right." *He frowned, soberly.* "It was me."

Luke: "Anyway. The idea was, that we would get Patrick and Louise to come back, you see, by going to her house and coming up with some lure about her sister. I think I said that Olivia was drunk and needed her help. I think that's sort of what I said. And the rest of us had to hide and wait. Then we would jump out and surprise them, when they arrived." *He lifted the can to his lips.* "It sounds very juvenile, but that's what we did."

Guy: "Except that Olivia was already gone."

Luke: "Are you absolutely sure?"

Guy: "Yes."

Narrator: "We just thought at first that she was hiding."

Luke: "But she wasn't."

A spotlight singles out Louise. And Louise takes up the story.

Louise: "Sometimes, personally I wonder that if we'd stayed at the bar whether any of this would have happened. They say it would and it's not like that. But I wonder if my sister would have gone to the moon. I know there's no use thinking, 'What if?' But you do. I ask myself that question all the time."

Luke: "I don't think that's worth it. Everything was fine."

Guy: "Anyway, we didn't leave her. She left us. Hasn't she always been like that?"

Narrator: "Whatever the reason was, by then she was gone. But we didn't know what had happened. I mean who would? Who would think that on an ordinary night their friend would go to the moon?"

Silence on stage as each character reflects on what happened.

Narrator: "When Guy came back, we jumped out, screaming and shouting. Then, when Olivia didn't appear, we started to search. We were all still smiling, because we thought she was hiding."

Luke: "And we were drunk."

Narrator: "But it stopped being funny. Searching was when we realised the grass had become clogged with water. So, we congregated on the bandstand. That's when we realised something was happening in the sky."

Guy & Luke: *The friends nod in agreement.*

Olivia: "I know what happened – " *The arrival of her voice surprises everyone. The lights now dim to Olivia, who we see on the bandstand. There is a plain look on her face. She sips calmly from a can of beer.*

Olivia: "There is a lot you see and think about that you don't tell anyone. Like in fact that what you think is for no one. And maybe not even for you. But you also think, that can't be true… what advantage would that have? If what you thought in your head wasn't for you? That would be as good as a reflection on the surface of a pond. Something that only God could be interested in." *Olivia stands and glances a moment to her right where Luke and Guy sit drunkenly. She then steps onto the grass, looks down at her feet, hesitates a moment before lifting her head. She begins to remember the events of that night.*

Olivia: "My foot landed with a squelch. And water rose out of the turf to cover my shoes. I smelt the air. And it was salty."

Guy: "She's a crazy bastard!"

Narrator: "The moon we looked up at was so large you couldn't believe your eyes. So brilliant that it was like looking into the sun. And a grey column of water rose to encircle it, forming a halo."

Louise: "Take a picture!"

Olivia: "I dived in and began to swim. I let my shoes fall off my feet. In the air a breeze. A strange churning, swirl of the water. And it got me. I rose onto a different plane. No longer did I seem to touch anything. I was flying. I was laughing. I knew somehow that it was going to be all right. My body got squeezed, like it was under barometric pressure." *Olivia clasps herself.* "Colour drained away. From there I don't remember a thing, until I woke up on the shore and they cut me out of the shell."

Narrator: "The barrier was white (she did not feel it – the mineral shell that formed around her bore the brunt). The speed at which she travelled meant she was gone."

Louise: "They took us away and asked us endless questions. They wanted to know everything. Exactly as it happened. Where we had been and what we had done. And all the thoughts we had shared."

Guy, Luke, Louise & Narrator: "All of us," *they say collectively.*

Narrator: "They went on and on about how important we were. As though it didn't matter that Olivia had gone to the moon. They called it 'Sky Water', which was the first time we'd heard those words."

One Month Later

"The official report on the young woman who came back from the moon: 'She returned to earth in an organic cask, like a permeable shell. We can only describe this shell as like a life-support machine or a womb, formed by the chemistry of heat, water, the mysterious behaviour of our collective unconscious and the gravitational pull of the moon.' It ferried her on a cartwheel and delivered her to the ocean, where she drifted ashore, like a foetal woman. What now, do we wonder, does the young woman know? How does she think? Can she tell us anything about the future of life on earth? She has been extensively interviewed and we have a short segment of that interview to broadcast tonight." *On the screen is projected the interview. But we see only Olivia's pale face.*

"Would it help if I told you the story of how I went to the moon?" *she asked, pre-empting the question.*

"Did you know at the time why you were there?"

"No."

"How did you eat and drink?"

"I didn't do either of those. The shell kept me alive. It was like being inside a lung. There was a gel inside it which filtered through my skin."

"Do you feel as though you've been altered?"

"No. Not in any way."

"Is there anything you have to tell us?"

"No. But I do have some thoughts."

"Can you tell us what those are, please?"

"Stop trying to escape."

"Why is that? From what? Is that a warning?"

"Terms of place apply to all living creatures all of the time. Where it is the animal gets born holds all of the animal's possibilities. Everything for every creature is possible. And all possible happiness is possible. Place is met in peace. They are our terms."

"That's everything?"

"Yes," *said Olivia.*

"Do you believe you have been brainwashed by an intelligent being?"

"No."

"Did the people on earth brainwash you?"

"Yes."

"Why would they do that?"

"Because they needed me to go to the moon."

"To your knowledge is an intelligent being coordinating these events?"

"No."

"How is that possible?"

"I don't know."

"Will all of us at some point go to the moon?"

"I hope so."

"But you don't know?"

"No."

"Did you want to go to the moon?"

"Yes."

"Why?"

(*No answer.*)

"Well, there you have it. If you were looking for answers, then you're probably disappointed. We go live for the last time to Carol on the street."

"Rick, you were shaking your head." Carol put it to her guest.

"Well. The girl's a loony and it's nonsense. It's a fake. The whole thing. If you believe any of this there's something wrong with you, seriously."

"You don't believe it happened?"

"Not for a second."

"Jana, you're here on holiday from Catalunya. Would you go to the moon?"

"Yes, really."

"You don't think this is a hoax, like Rick?"

"No. Why would you say that?"

"Rick?"

"People will believe anything these days."

"Back to you."

The newsreader holds a page in his hands.

"Let me just offer you these words, that whatever fate has in store for us, whatever you need to know, you'll learn about here on our programme. Goodnight, I hope you sleep well, and we'll see you tomorrow."

The programme credits rolled.

END of Act 3, Scene 3

"It was really good," said Madeline. He looked at her and saw there was a tear in her eye.

Without time to react, Latham jumped on stage, the polite applause from the audience yet to end.

"Thank you to our cast and all their efforts, our director and our head of the English department, Mr Eric Crawford. We would like you all to stay for a brief address from patron of the arts, Miss Francesca Crawford." They watched, with anticipation, as Francesca got up from her chair, and climbed to the stage.

"Thank you," she said. "Well. I came here to see the play. It's one thing when your son's in a school play; it's another when he writes it. For all of those reasons, I don't want to say very much. What I will say simply is that I believe the arts are the best chance we have. My warmest congratulations to the cast for a wonderful and provocative play. I won't say any more. Please, enjoy your evening. I'm very pleased to have been invited." She went to leave.

"Does anyone have any questions?" asked Latham.

"I really didn't want to do anything like that," said Francesca.

"Sam," continued Latham and pointed.

"I was wondering if you could tell us what's happening to Maja and Elias?" asked Sam. Francesca was alert to mobile phones.

"Well, look, as I said, I had no intention of talking tonight. A lot of people are already involved, and certainly the press love to hound me about it. Look, let me be cryptic. I've learned this year to weigh the cost of my pleasure. It's a wake-up call. Maja and Elias asked me for my help to articulate their point. So, I'm trying to do that."

But already on course to interrupt the evening were airborne globules of paint. The shock tactic landing to splatter the stage. To climb the hem of Francesca's dress, and to plant their kiss on her cheek. The reaction from the seated audience was uproar, as everyone jumped to their feet, Adrian and Eric outpaced by the police, who grabbed someone and then bundled them out.

"It's all right," announced Francesca. "I'm getting used to it." She was then herself led from the stage.

In what seemed like just a moment all was calm again. Albeit, of course, presenting a radically different situation.

Eric stood outside, contemplating the fresh wreckage. Without knowing whether to do so, he walked out through the college gate to sit in the car. Seeing then how he had outpaced everyone. Because from behind the windscreen, he watched Georgina, a foot taller than Madeline, carry off his script. He let them go.

Once the exodus had passed, Eric got out again and returned to the hall. The stage curtains hung half-closed. Chairs scattered. He sat down where he'd sat before, his chair miraculously just where he'd left it; something in the air perhaps. He cast his eyes over the disruption.

"Eric," said the Storyteller.

"Yes," said Eric.

"Is everything all right?"

"Yes, fine. Thank you," said Eric. He sat there, his eyes falling on the now-smeared and trodden-in trail of paint. He found himself, next, standing beside the stage. He put his palm flat into the sticky pigment, long enough to feel the sensation of its silky adhesiveness. The police returned, at that moment, equipped to document the scene. "We're cordoning off this area, sir." An officer with a camera began snapping. Eric took his cue.

"I don't know how much the college can take of this," said Latham, looking up from his phone. A phalanx of police vehicles, the boys in blue, escorting the last of their guests.

Eric got into the burgundy car, marking the steering wheel with yellow paint, and drove home.

32

Knock, knock.

"Eric Crawford?"

"Yes?"

"DC Bradbury and this is DC Collins. We'd like to ask you some questions in relation to events last night at Davenport College."

"Please, come in." Eric stood aside.

"We'd rather discuss this at the station," said the officer.

"Okay. Let me change." The two officers made their way to the car. Eric then sat himself in the back seat.

"All right?" DC Bradbury looked at him.

"Yes." Eric nodded. In the interview room they supplied him with a Styrofoam cup of black tea.

"Quite a night."

"Yes," agreed Eric.

"We've arrested one of your students," said DC Bradbury. "It's becoming something of a habit," he said. "Arresting your students."

"Who was it?" asked Eric.

"Sam Honeywell."

"I'm very surprised," said Eric. "He's a level-headed student."

"Well, he will be interviewed, and we'll find out. But we're here to talk to you, Mr Crawford. Frankly, because you keep coming to our attention. You know as a result of what happened during David Spurling's trial, that we've been making further enquiries."

"Yes," said Eric. "But David was never one of my students. I've had very little contact with him."

"Well, yes, up to a point that seems to be the case. We know that you taught David as a supply teacher during the summer of 2009."

"I don't see how that's relevant."

"We don't actually think that it is. But it's a fact, Mr Crawford. Are you aware, Mr Crawford, that hospitals now have an obligation, when a non-relative or non-guardian attends hospital with a minor, to pass that person's details to the police?"

"No."

"Well, it is. Interviews have to be taken from all medical staff. DC Collins is going to show you a photograph. Do you recognise these individuals?"

"Yes," said Eric. Eric looked down at a picture of the two clowns outside the hospital.

"Were you aware they were friends of David's?"

"No. I'd never met them before."

"We see them handing you a piece of paper. What is that, please?"

"It's a flyer."

"Do you still have it?"

"Yes, I think so," said Eric.

"We'd like to have that. At the trial you denied any connection with The Wednesday Group?"

"Yes."

"Does your mother have any connection with The Wednesday Group?"

"No. Not that I'm aware of," said Eric.

"And what about this Swedish pair, Maja and Elias?"

"I don't know."

"Okay. Take a look at this for us, if you will." They put David's letter on the table, encased in a transparent plastic bag.

"Did you notice anything strange about it?"

"No," said Eric.

"Okay." DC Bradbury placed in front of him an annotated version, the first letter of each sentence circled.

"What about now?" Eric looked. The circled letters, when combined, repeated the word 'Wednesday'.

"Do you see that?"

"Yes," confirmed Eric.

"What does it spell?"

"It spells 'Wednesday'."

"Which we think is a reference to The Wednesday Group. Therefore, the question we have for you, Eric, is why would David send you a coded message unless you understood the code?"

"I don't know," said Eric. "Isn't it a game?"

"You appreciate why we would ask?"

"Yes, of course."

"It seems reasonable to you?"

"Yes."

"It's strong circumstantial evidence." DC Bradbury looked at him. "Why would a seventeen-year-old boy try to recruit a forty-two-year-old man? It just doesn't sound plausible, does it? You see, we have no doubt that David knew exactly what he was doing when he opened the gas valves. The outstanding question is whether he acted alone."

"Who knows what was going on in his mind?" said Eric.

"Do you really believe that, Mr Crawford?"

"I gave you the letter," said Eric.

"Yes, you did. It was also logged by the prison officials. You see, Mr Crawford, the more we look the more we find. You appear to us to be a charismatic teacher with a strong connection to David Spurling. You worked in the building he destroyed. You appear to have an affiliation with the protest movement. There's the letter, and there's your mother's connection. A high-profile figure, who happens to be involved in a public campaign. How much circumstantial evidence does it take? We'd like you to watch this, Mr Crawford. You appear in the footage at 16:49. If we play it forwards, you'll see a young woman jump the metal barricade. When she stands up, she appears to recognise you. Do you know this young woman? Her name is Beth Hargrove and she's the regional organiser of which group, do you think? We checked your computer for its browsing history, which shows you visited The Wednesday Group's site. We think there's a compelling story here. So, we ask you, Mr Crawford, are you abusing your position as a teacher at Davenport College? Is your role as a teacher just a front?"

There was a knock at the interview room door.

"Guv?"

"All right. Mr Crawford, I'm going to transfer you to a cell for your own safety."

They led Eric to a cell down the corridor. There, Eric watched the door close behind him. He sat down on the bunk and laced his fingers. The effect of the strong tea prompted him to relieve himself. While he stood emptying his bladder his eyes surveyed the graffiti on the wall. One such example being a telephone with a button for 'Room Service'. Seated on the bunk, he cast his head upwards and pushed his glasses over the bridge of his nose.

"Eric?" interjected the voice of the Storyteller.

"Yes?"

"You realise the choice you made."

"Yes," said Eric.

"Like your mother," said the Storyteller.

"Uh huh," said Eric. He hesitated a moment. "Look," said Eric, "am I really involved in this or not?"

"It's really up to you," said the Storyteller. Twenty minutes later, and Eric watched the cell door reopen.

"We're very sorry about that," he said. They took Eric home. There Eric stood against the back door and smoked.

"Where were you? I've been trying to get hold of you," said Madeline.

"I was at the police station. They had some questions for me."

"Do I need to get you a solicitor, Eric?"

"No. I don't think so. I think they were just making a point."

33

"Well, we did, it didn't we?" said the Storyteller.

"I suppose," said Eric. "I'm not entirely clear about it. Did we save the future?"

"I think so."

"I'm your hero then," said Eric.

"We have to keep telling this story forever," said the Storyteller. Eric nods.

"It's fate," the Storyteller continued.

"Right. So, is that it then?" asked Eric.

"Yes. I think so. Do you know," said the Storyteller, changing the subject, "how we know what other people feel?"

"No, not really," said Eric.

"It's facial muscles. We imitate expressions. And from the imitation, you feel what the other person feels. Isn't that strange?"

"I agree it's not what you'd think," said Eric.

"What would you think?"

"Well, that it would come from inside you."

"I think we've found out that words are the same. Our identities form around them. The inside is really outside. And did you know," the Storyteller changed tack again, "that it's my birthday tomorrow?" The writer began tidying up his desk. "I'll be sixty. And I'll be retiring." He looked up. "Grace is throwing me a party."

"Happy birthday," said Eric.

"Thank you."

"What are you going to do about the speech?" Eric asked.

"Oh, I have that," smiled the writer. "It's all worked out now, thank you, Eric. I'm going to tell people the truth."

"And what about the book?"

"That's finished too. You finished your play. I finished my book. It was very good," said the Storyteller. "It was very good indeed. But I suppose now I'd better go, Eric," he said.

Eric nodded. "Okay. Good luck."

"And you," said the Storyteller. The Storyteller reached out calmly and switched off the light.

———•———

A bustle of party guests swept in to crowd the Storyteller's house. It was his sixtieth birthday and lots of his and Grace's friends came. Other writers he was friends with, people from the publishing world. A flock of chatter.

"Where have you been? I've missed you," they gushed. And Grace, well, she looked beautiful. The Storyteller moved about the house. It was cocktail hour.

"What is it about?" Max cornered him. Max, his diligent editor, who was always working.

"It's," the Storyteller began, "a story about a man trying to write a story about a story he can't write." That kept Max quiet.

"And how's the speech?"

"I've got it right here." He tapped his temple. "And here," he said, pointing to the brown envelope on his desk.

After their guests had left, he sat with Grace in the living room. It was early the next morning.

"Leave it until tomorrow," he said, looking at the mess.

"Today, you mean," Grace smiled.

"Thank you for a wonderful party."

"Well, I think you deserved it," she said. "After all the hard work you've put in."

"I couldn't have done it without you."

"What did Max want?" she asked.

"Oh, you know."

"Have you told him?" she asked. He looked at her.

"No, not yet. I will. I know. You're right." He took a mouthful of water.

"Are you ready? For tomorrow?"

"You mean for today," he smiled. He reached out for the envelope.

"Let's try and get some sleep," she said.

The green door at the back of the garden opened onto a discreet passageway. The advantage, therefore, that you could set out whenever you wanted, unobserved. Something which helped him remain in a preparatory state. He pushed his hand to delicately close the gate. The channel quiet. The familiar narrow stretch of nettles and wildflowers. He blinked, touched his chin, checked his glasses, one polished shoe proceeding to follow the other. Not yet any distinct or palpable sense of occasion. At times like these he tried to remain in control of himself. That was where June came in. It had never appealed to him to walk into Laureate Square alone. And for reasons he had never deigned to fathom (probably to do with ego) it could not be with Grace.

The spot where he usually met June was outside a grand house they'd chosen for the occasion on Caleb Street. That was where they would rendezvous, as though just another couple on their way to hear what the City Laureate had to say. That is to say, their story began there. Today he lifted his collar. Two more streets. And then June. The safety of June. She stood in recognisable profile, her neck wrapped in a scarf. She waved when she saw him. To which, in reply, he lifted the brown envelope and waved back. This was their brand of semaphore. You see, it was innocence personified.

"Hello," she said. That scarf around her neck. And then, "How are you feeling?" she asked.

"Oh, all right," he said.

"Remember, it's just another one." He looked at her.

"How's Grace?"

"Oh, fine," the Storyteller said. And when they got to the square it was, as it always was, brimming with people. Maybe they knew after all? And quickly, thereafter, he was spotted on the path to the lectern, prompting in the air a swell of applause. The lectern was mounted on a simple makeshift stage, which got rolled out each year. From there the Storyteller knew it was theatre. He left June's arm, waved to the crowd, bringing himself to order by removing the pages and setting them down.

"Good afternoon," he said, his voice amplified. He looked out at his audience and smiled, letting the secondary applause quieten. "I have something different to tell you this year. I hope you appreciate it. It's a confession and it's in two parts. But first I have to tell you a fact about this year. This year you've been sending me letters and they tell me I have forgotten something about storytelling. And you're right. I agree with you. I don't know how many of you are here today who wrote me these letters, but I've written this speech for you. But I hope it will mean something to all of you." The Storyteller leant into the microphone tentatively. "I know it's very cold, and I won't keep you," he said. "This is my first confession." The Storyteller cleared his throat.

"'I woke up this morning and felt something very strange, as if something was missing. Did you? Maybe you did too?' It was a feeling he couldn't put his finger on. He pulled back the curtain, then went downstairs to open the front door. He put a disturbed hand to his disturbed face. Where was he exactly?

"'Love?' she called after him.

"'You all right, Harry?' his neighbour enquired.

"'I…' he began to say but left it unsaid. He protested to his wife that he had to go into the city. He took with him paper and pen. He went about the churches but did not find what he was looking for there. He followed the people dressed for work but did not find it with them either. He stopped a young woman to ask her what was going on, but he didn't understand what she said. All, in fact, that proved familiar to him were the birds in the sky. He stood, cast in the street, wearing pyjamas.

"'I don't know,' his wife said, calling their son, 'he's just gone out. I can't call the police because the old fool doesn't know what to do with himself. You know, he's been like this ever since he retired. I know. But what do you do? Yes. I'll try,' she said and put down the receiver.

"This, then, is my second and final confession. It's set in a city where you can tell stories. It's what I really want to tell you," he said. "This is about two friends, a man named Ernesto and a man named Santiago. Both men the sons of families that migrated to America. I hope they will become your friends too. They are New Yorkers. And weekends they play chess in Bryant Park. Theirs is a cold day in New York City. Much like ours is today. And so, Ernesto and Santiago wear thick hats and gloves as they move their chess pieces. When Ernesto told Santiago, which he did frequently, how difficult it was for him to make a living, his friend usually came up with a dismissive remark. Today it was no different. Or at least that's what Santiago thought.

"'Gee-whiz, it's just the Storyteller,' he said.

"'Who?' said Ernesto.

"'What?' said Santiago. 'You don't know who the Storyteller is?'

"'No. I never heard of him.'

"'You never heard of him!' exclaimed Santiago. 'How can you not know who the Storyteller is? Have you got your fingers in your ears? It's like you don't know who your parents are!'

"'Okay. Well, tell me. Who is the Storyteller?' said Ernesto.

"'He's like responsible for us, look around.'

"'Me?' asked Ernesto, his brow creased with confusion.

"'Yeah. I mean, it's where we come from. It's why we're here.' Ernesto looked down at the table.

"'You know when you see that guy,' said Santiago, 'up there. And your mind gets,' he gesticulated, 'like, ah… squeezed up? And then all filled up with stuff. Like the content of your thoughts.'

"'Yeah…'

"'Well, that's who you meet. That's the Storyteller. He tells us who we are. But you don't remember. Or if you do, it's, I don't know, easy to forget.'

"'How come nobody said before?'

"'How do I know?' said Santiago.

A week later, at two o'clock in the afternoon, Santiago and Ernesto were playing their usual game.

"'You know I hear there's some new character, a teacher, he's working with,' said Ernesto, eager to demonstrate that he understood.

"'Uh huh,' replied Santiago.

"'They say it's gonna be a real tall tale. Bigger than anything he's written before'

"'Look do you mind? You're distracting me. Do you want to win or lose? Here. Check.'

"'I could see you were gonna do that.'

"'Oh, could you?'

"'Yeah.'

"'Well, big shot. What are you gonna do about it?' Ernesto studied the arrangement.

The week after that, in the midst of their game, Ernesto said to Santiago, 'I was looking up there the other day and you know, the place looked empty.'

"'Everybody can have a holiday,' said Santiago.

"'No,' said Ernesto. 'It was different. I don't think the Storyteller was there.'

"'Don't be ridiculous. Make your move.'

"'I'm being serious, I think he's gone.'

"'He can't go. He has to be there.'

"'Well, I think he has.' As the two characters looked at one another an eerie sense came over them. They didn't know what to call it. If it was fear, then it didn't explain why they were both smiling.

"'What are you thinking?' asked Ernesto. Santiago just shrugged.

"'I don't know.' And then, with his usual brio, 'Make your move,' said Santiago."

The Storyteller collected his pages and left the stage.

This book is printed on paper from sustainable sources managed under the Forest Stewardship Council (FSC) scheme.

It has been printed in the UK to reduce transportation miles and their impact upon the environment.

For every new title that Matador publishes, we plant a tree to offset CO_2, partnering with the More Trees scheme.

For more about how Matador offsets its environmental impact, see www.troubador.co.uk/about/